TABLE OF CONTENTS

TITLE PAGE
COPYRIGHT
CHAPTER ONE
CHAPTER TWO
CHAPTER THREE
CHAPTER FOUR
CHAPTER FIVE
CHAPTER SIX
CHAPTER SEVEN
CHAPTER EIGHT
CHAPTER NINE
CHAPTER TEN
CHAPTER ELEVEN
CHAPTER TWELVE
CHAPTER THIRTEEN
CHAPTER FOURTEEN
READ AN EXCERPT OF BEAUTIFUL LIAR
ACKNOWLEDGMENTS
ABOUT ZARA COX
OTHER BOOKS BY ZARA COX

WRECKLESS

BY

ZARA COX

Copyright © 2013 Zara Cox

Cover by Angela Oltmann

All rights reserved. No part of this e-book may be reproduced in any form other than that in which it was purchased and without the written permission of the author.

This is a work of fiction. Names, characters, places, brands, media, and incidents are either the product of the author's imagination or are used fictitiously. Any resemblance to actual events, locales, or persons, living or dead, is coincidental.

This e-book is licensed for your personal enjoyment only.

This e-book may not be re-sold or given away to other people. If you would like to share this book with another person, please purchase an additional copy for each recipient. If you're reading this book and did not purchase it, or it was not purchased for your use only, then please return it to the retailer and purchase your own copy. Thank you for respecting the hard work of this author.

Chapter One

Early Spring 2012

"C'mon, ladies, bottoms up!"

"Bottoms up? The way you're going, it'll be bottoms *out* before the hour's up!" Lexi Mayfield shouted over the sound of pumping music to her friend and bachelorette party honoree, Cara Saldana.

"That's fine by me. I have a very nice ass, so if it wants to hang out, I just might let it." The statuesque brunette rose, planted red-tipped fingers on the table, and performed an exquisite little wriggle with said ass, earning several appreciative whistles from the guys at a nearby bar. Fiona and Sally, the other two girls forming their quartet, giggled and joined in the dance. One sported a cheeky veil and the other a red halo. The catcalls grew louder, and Lexi watched the girls, buoyed by countless cosmopolitans, start an impromptu conga line around the table.

Friday night, and *Manjaro's*, the latest "in" club on the London social scene, was packed to the rafters. From their center booth, Lexi observed the beautiful and not-so-beautiful drink, dance, and flirt, wishing she'd gone with her original suggestion of a spa weekend to treat her soon-to-be married friend.

Nightclubs weren't her thing, especially the headache-inducing strobe lights and the head-banging shriek-fest that passed for music. *Manjaro's*, as she'd rightly predicted, was a wall-to-wall meat market. Guys in tight fitting clothes - some showing off honed muscles, others desperately hiding paunches - performed improbable gymnastics to the throbbing music, alongside women in skimpy outfits. She grimaced, looked away, and shuddered as the short, comb-over guy at the next table gave her a lecherous once-over.

Give her a salsa club with soft lights and sensual Latin music any day. Or better yet, the serene bliss of her favorite spa, which is where she planned to celebrate her own bachelorette party in a month's time.

The now much longer conga line approached. Cara, self-appointed fearless leader, whooped and swayed in front, leading ardent followers between the tables.

"Come on, Lexi." She made a grab for her as they passed by the table.

"No, thanks. I'm fine exactly where I am, thanks." Lord, she hated making a spectacle of herself. Joining the conga line clad in the short, tight black mini skirt Cara had all but forced her into was definitely out of the question.

She cringed as Cara stopped, hands planted on her hips and glared at her. "You promised, Lexi. You promised me a fantastic time tonight. These are my last days of freedom, for fuck's sake! The least you can do is help me enjoy myself."

Lexi refrained from reminding her semi-inebriated friend that she didn't need anyone to have a good time. Cara could have a full-blown party in a padded cell all by herself.

Instead, she put down her mineral water and let herself be pulled up, her protests ignored as Cara forced her in front of the line.

"Finally, some signs of life! Now wriggle that ass and show me what makes my big brother so hot for you," she commanded.

"*Cara!*"

"Oh, don't be such a prude," Cara replied, her American accent distinctive in the jumbled mix of Cockney and middle-class tones. Her hands slid up over Lexi's hips and anchored at her waist. "What is it you English say? Don't be such a big girl's blouse? Now move!"

Pushed from behind by the restless line, Lexi stumbled forward, going with the sway of bodies. She opened her mouth to explain that the expression was normally reserved for wimpy *men* not women, but stopped as she felt Cara's warm breath tease her ear.

"Don't think I haven't heard you and Enzo going at it like crazed monkeys. You don't fool me for a second with that

Mary Poppins facade. Underneath those don't-touch-me clothes, you're a raging little vixen."

Lexi turned shocked eyes to her friend, frantically trying to recall when Cara could have heard her with Enzo. It must've been—

"Yep, the night of your birthday party last month," Cara supplied helpfully. "You guys thought I'd left. I'd crashed in the back bedroom. Your screams woke me up. For such a prude, you're very…vocal in bed, aren't you? Or was it your brand new status as my brother's fiancée that got you so hot?" Her crude chuckle grated on Lexi's nerves.

"Sorry if the noise woke you…" She flinched as the hand around her waist tightened almost painfully.

"If that's your thing, then go for it, I say. As long as you think you're doing the right thing, that is."

"The right thing? You mean marrying your brother?" The loud music made her think she'd misheard, but when she glanced over her shoulder, the look in Cara's eyes told a different story. Lexi tried not to react to the mild venom she saw there.

"It's easy to confuse great sex with love. And as much as I love him, Enzo can be a jerk sometimes. Besides, he's not exactly the homebody type. He works really long hours. Hell, sometimes he doesn't come home at all, just sleeps at his club, and not always alone, if you know what I mean. You sure you want to put up with that?"

Lexi frowned as alarm skated down her spine. "Should you talk about your brother that way?" She tried to pull away.

Cara stayed right behind her. "He's *my* brother; I'm stuck with him." She paused a beat. "But there's no reason why you should be."

Lexi missed a step and stumbled as the restless dancers pushed the conga line forward. "Are you trying to tell me something? Are you warning me off?" Were the fears she'd harbored since becoming engaged to Enzo real? Did Cara hate the thought of her, or anyone else for that matter, marrying her precious brother?

The younger woman gave a shrug. "I just think all this happened too fast. Maybe you need to think about it some more before you rush into a mistake you'll regret."

"The same way you rushed into your engagement to Ian after only three weeks?"

Her hands dropped from Lexi's waist and she stopped in the middle of the dance floor. "You think I'm making a mistake? Or are you jealous because Ian asked *me* to marry him even though you dated him first?"

"I'm not jealous and I never said you were making a mistake, but obviously you think *I* am by marrying *your* brother."

Cara's lips turned downward. "Maybe I'm giving you advice that I hope my own brother would give me if he thought I was making a mistake."

"And does he?"

"No, he knows I'm happy with Ian."

"And I'm happy with your brother, so let's drop this, shall we?" For several seconds, the mutinous expression remained in Cara's eyes. "Cara?"

"Hey, what's the holdup? Let's keep the conga movin'!" someone shouted from behind.

"Fine, just make sure you're doing the right thing, considering your age and all." Undisguised malice accompanied the words and Lexi's heart sank even further.

"Gee thanks, but I don't think twenty-nine qualifies me for the recycling dump just yet."

Cara flicked back her hair, shameless at her insult. "You know what I mean."

"No, I don't. And frankly, I don't think I *want* to know." When Cara tried to force Lexi to resume the conga, she pulled away. "I think I'll go and sit down now."

Heart pounding, she returned to the table and swallowed a mouthful of mineral water. While it wet her throat, she couldn't help but wish for something stronger to dull the edge of her anxiety.

As designated driver, however, she had no choice but to stick to water. Unfortunately, it did nothing to stop the fretful emotions rampaging through her.

Because somewhere in the recesses of her mind, she'd also questioned how she, a snuggie-and-X-Factor-loving, nightclub-loathing nobody like her had managed to bag someone like Enzo Saldana, the sexiest man she'd ever seen?

Yeah, the thought had intruded once or twice, way before Cara's brazen put down.

Breathing deep, Lexi placed the glass on the table and paused as she caught sight of her engagement ring.

Enzo.

Just the mere thought of him calmed her nerves.

Enzo, the love of her life. Her other half. Her soul mate.

God, she hadn't believed such intense feelings could exist between two human beings until she met him.

Four weeks ago, after only three months of dating, he'd asked her to marry him, and all her dreams had come true. Eastwell Manor was booked, courtesy of a last-minute cancellation, and her fairytale dress now hung in her closet.

In two months' time, she'd walk down the aisle, join her life with Lorenzo Saldana's, and live happily fucking ever after.

A smile broke over her face. All of a sudden, she couldn't wait to get back home, coax him round to her apartment, and have monkey sex with him.

God bless the day Sally had talked her into joining her salsa class.

She'd spied Enzo the minute she'd walked into the salsa club on the third week of lessons--a dark, brooding figure in the corner of the main bar. Having already met him and received his frosty reception at the house she'd showed to him and his sister that morning, she'd been reluctant to approach him again, even though his eyes remained pinned on her. She'd watched surreptitiously as he rebuffed all attempts from the women in the class to seduce him onto the dance floor.

Tall, sleekly-muscled, clad in jeans and a tight black T-shirt, the word *smoldering* seemed to sum up the raven-haired hunk who'd watched with lazy amusement as she attempted the complicated salsa moves.

In the end, she suspected that he'd taken over her practice out of pity as she'd tortured the dance steps.

But all it'd taken was one touch, one look into his deep, green eyes, and she'd lost her heart. Well that, and him molding her to his body halfway through a particularly sensual move, fisting one strong hand in her hair and whispering hotly in her ear, "*I'm not sure whether I want to teach you how to salsa properly or just take you home and fuck you ten ways to heaven.*"

"Take me home," she'd whispered with an urgency that had shocked her.

He'd taken her home. He'd showed her exactly *one* salsa move. Then he'd thrown her on the floor and fucked her until she was hoarse from screaming her pleasure.

By morning, she'd been halfway in love with him, swept away by feelings so strong, Mount Vesuvius at full rage couldn't have stopped her from claiming him as hers.

That he felt the same made heaven a truly wonderful, glorious place to be.

Except for the snake in paradise.

From the start of her relationship with Enzo, Lexi had felt Cara's mild disapproval. She couldn't pinpoint the problem because they'd seem to hit it off after being introduced by Lexi's childhood friend, Sally. Cara hero-worshiped her brother, that much had been obvious from the get-go.

But lately, she'd begun to wonder whether Cara had faked her goodwill. With her stark warning just now, Lexi could no longer pretend that she had Cara's blessing. But why did she hate the idea of her marrying Enzo so much? Couldn't she see how happy she made Enzo, and vice versa?

Lexi's solitaire ring glinted in the strobe lights of the club, and her warm glow receded as she recalled how disastrous her previous relationships had been.

Take Ian, for instance. Contrary to Cara's inference that she was jealous, she'd felt nothing but relief when Ian had turned his attentions to someone else. Although they'd dated for a while, Lexi had never felt he was *the one*. And frankly by the time she broke things off, Ian's intensity had scared her a little.

Cara had struck a nerve, calling her a prude. Or at least that'd been the label hung on her before Enzo had shown her that there was more to sex than vanilla-missionary with her eyes shut in the dark. Hell, he'd even taught her that gentle loving could also be red-hot. Sex with Ian had always left her feeling inadequate and unfulfilled.

With Enzo, she'd discovered the true meaning of coital bliss.

A tingle shimmered through her and her nipples puckered as she recalled their session just this afternoon, the power of his relentless demand as he'd slammed his thick cock inside her. But more than that it was the way he'd vocalized his pleasure that made sex with Enzo so hot.

The dramatic cut of her blue silk halter-top had meant no bra tonight and the material chafed with a delicious pleasure-pain sensation, which causing her to bite her lip. Warmth flooded Lexi's face as she acknowledged that no matter how often she made love with him, she always yearned for his touch. Enzo had become her drug and she'd given up ever getting him out of her system. The moment she thought about him, she craved him. And as she'd come to realize, there would be no relief from that craving until she received what she wanted - him between her legs.

She shifted in her seat, desperate to ease the swirling heat in her pelvis. The seam of her thong pressed against her clit, the damp material causing delicious friction. A moan escaped, but the sound was thankfully swallowed by the loud music. Eyes shut, she took a deep, restorative breath. Another hour, give or take, and she'd be with Enzo. He'd ease her need and make things right.

As for Cara…

The shout of the returning conga line ended her thoughts. She arranged a presentable smile on her face, pressed her thighs together to stem the throbbing, and looked up as Cara plopped down on her seat. The silver and jade beads of her long necklace swung over the bosom of her tight green tube dress.

"Ready to leave?" Lexi asked the trio of sweaty, smiling women.

Fiona, the pint-sized, blonde American friend of Cara's, reached for the pitcher and poured drinks. "Not yet. I need to cool down a bit first. That guy I was dancing with sure sent my temperature soaring. Woohoo." She fanned herself with one hand and tipped her glass to her lips with the other.

"Yeah, his hand soared all the way up your top," Sally grinned, flicking her black hair off her shoulders and reaching for her drink.

"He was just making sure his number was stored in a safe, secure place." Fiona grinned back, batting false eyelashes.

"That rules out your panties, then, doesn't it?" Cara winked at her.

"It would've, if I wore any," Fiona shot back.

The table erupted in hoots of shocked laughter, and Lexi couldn't hold back her grin. As much as she would've preferred the spa, she was glad to see the girls enjoying themselves.

When they tottered off for one last dance, Lexi pulled out her cell phone and saw Enzo's text.

How much longer, baby? E

Smiling, she responded. *Another half hour. Your place or mine?*

He responded within seconds. The thought that he'd been waiting for her to get in touch thrilled her.

Mine. Hurry. Been thinking of you all night. Dying for you to come home and fuck me. Dying for you to use that gorgeous mouth on me, make me come harder than ever.

Heat engulfed her. God, she loved him, especially when he didn't hold back about what he wanted from her! And hell yeah, she loved his thick, beautiful cock too.

Be there soon. Promise xx

She thought of saying more, of vocalizing what she wanted but she wasn't quite there yet even though she let him coax her every now and then...

Biting her lip, she put the phone away.

"Right, shall we go?" she asked as soon as the girls returned from the dance floor, itching to be away.

"No!" Cara protested. "Five more minutes, please?" she pleaded, and gulped down another drink.

Biting back her irritation, Lexi succumbed. "Okay, five minutes, but no more." It was almost three o'clock in the morning, and she'd had enough.

She wanted Enzo. Knowing he was waiting for her made sitting still near impossible. But she gritted her teeth and fixed a smile on her face.

"I know what we can do. Truth or dare. One question each. Then we'll leave. Deal?" Cara asked, earning rapturous enthusiasm from the other two. But she didn't look at them. She stared straight at Lexi.

Foreboding crept up her spine.

"Umm, I don't think—"

"Exactly, *don't think*. Just play. Okay?" Cara dared.

Before she could respond, Fiona piped up, "Okay, I'll go first. Someone ask me."

"Right," Sally jumped in. "Truth or dare."

"Dare, *always*," Fiona replied.

"Fabulous! I fucking dare you to go flash your tits at that bald guy sitting at the bar."

"Done!" Giggling, she rose on unsteady feet, sashayed to the man in question, leaned down, and whispered in his ear. He shot up from his seat, eyes wide, and nodded eagerly. Fiona yanked up her top, giving him, and everyone else in the vicinity, an eyeful of her bountiful, braless breasts. Throaty wolf whistles and pleas for an *encore* followed her back to the table.

"That was exhilarating. I *love* English guys! Can I do it again?" she begged, licking her full lips.

Cara shook her head. "No, you shameless slut. You're in town for my wedding, not to get laid every other night. You're only limited to one flash," she grinned. "Now, my turn. *I*, too, will take a dare, if you please."

Whoops erupted round the table and Lexi cringed at the brazen look in Cara's eyes.

"Okaaay," Sally looked around. "I dare you to do whatever it takes to get a hundred quid from that guy over there with the pouting blonde."

"Sally!"

"Oh relax, Lexi, it's just a game," Sally remonstrated.

"Yeah, stop getting your thong in a twist, girlfriend, and watch a professional at work," Cara chided.

Pulling out her compact mirror from her purse, Cara checked her appearance, and tweaked a few hairs. She pushed back her shoulders to display even more of her D-cups, stood up and with casual ease strode toward the blonde entwined around her target.

She tapped the girl on the shoulder. When she had her attention, she leaned up to the taller woman and whispered in her ear. The girl jerked back, surprise in her eyes as her mouth dropped open. She leaned over and spoke to her boyfriend. A broad smile broke over his face and he whispered back. The blonde's wary stare at her boyfriend gradually turned sensuous and, with a slow sexy smile, she handed her glass to him, turned to Cara and nodded.

Cara stepped closer, ran one hand up the blonde's arm until she cupped her shoulder. She squeezed gently, then continued the trail up to slide around her nape. Gliding her other hand around her waist, she pulled the blonde closer and covered her mouth in a sensual kiss.

For several seconds, the kiss went on and, even though the others couldn't see her, Lexi tried not to cringe at such a public display. As much as she hated the prude label and wanted rid of it, she knew she would never have enough confidence to discard her inhibitions long enough to participate in such a voyeuristic act.

While the other girls giggled uncontrollably at the outrageous floorshow, she fixed a smile on her face and cringed inwardly.

When the two finally parted, she breathed a sigh of guilty relief. Cara sauntered back to the table, triumphantly holding up the money the boyfriend had coughed up.

She slapped it on the table and turned to Lexi. "Your turn."

"No, I'll go last. Sally, truth or dare," she asked, and prayed her friend wouldn't go for the latter. She couldn't stand another floorshow like the last one, and she'd had enough of being called a prude for one night.

"Truth."

Relief eased through her.

"Okay. Something I've always wondered," Cara broke in, her feverish gaze raking Lexi's face before returning to Sally. "Have you and Lexi ever slept together?"

Sally splattered her drink all over the table, surprise plastered on her model-thin face. "*Are you kidding?* I always have and always will prefer my bed partners with a whole lot of meat between their legs. So does Lexi, I believe." She winked at Lexi and took another sip of her drink.

"And last but not least, Lexi. Truth or dare?" Fiona asked.

She bit her lip, knowing she was caught between the proverbial rock and a hard place. There was no way she'd take a dare after seeing what the other two had entailed; but the avid faces of the other three girls told her whatever truth she'd be asked to reveal would be very personal and very sexual. She'd look like a spoilt sport if she chickened out. "Truth," she all but whispered.

Cara pounced before anyone else could. "Have you ever fantasized about being fucked in a very public place, maybe with other people watching?" She grinned at the gasps around the table. "I just, you know…wondered, you being such a prude and all."

Lexi froze. Somehow, Cara had tapped into her deepest, wildest fantasy. She knew she talked a lot when she was drunk. The last time she'd been off her face had been at her birthday party. Had she blurted out her secret then, at the one occasion when she'd drank way more than was good for her?

After years of being called a prude, she'd often wondered if she was perhaps too conservative when it came to sex. With Enzo, she'd begun to think she wasn't, but for years she'd fantasized about what it would be like to break out of her shell sexually. And the one recurring fantasy she'd had was of being fucked in a public place, where all the guys who'd mocked her inhibitions could see her and regret their name-calling. But how the fuck had Cara known?

"Come on, Lexi, we're waiting. *Truth, truth, truth, truth,*" the girls chanted.

She bit her lip. "Okay, okay. Yes, I've…thought about it, I guess. No more than anyone else, I'm sure."

"And?" Cara pressed, as she took another healthy slug of her drink.

Lexi shrugged self-consciously. "And nothing. I've only thought about it."

"W-would you like to?" Cara slurred.

"Stop it, Cara, now you've got her all hot and bothered. Here, Lexi, have a drink, calm your nerves." Sally shoved a cocktail glass in her hand.

"No, I'm driving, remember?"

"Fuck it, one little drink won't hurt. Besides I'd rather have you driving with calm nerves than all twisted up the way you are now," she teased. "God, you'd think we've asked you whether you love anal."

Jesus. Sometimes, she wondered why she called these girls her friends.

"Fine." Willing her cheeks to stop burning, she grabbed the glass and downed the mouthful. The unexpected heat of the vodka worked its way down her throat. Grimacing at the tartness of the cranberry juice, she set the glass down and looked up to find Cara's gaze on her.

"So-o you gonna anssswer my question?"

Not in this lifetime. "No more questions. I've played the game, fair and square. Now, I think it's time to go." Hurriedly she stood, gathered the purses and handbags, and busied herself with making sure the tab was settled. All the while, she felt Cara's drunken gaze on her. Without looking her way again, she led the other two girls out into the pre-dawn air. She paused, inhaled a welcome breath of fresh air, only to have it whoosh out of her when slim arms closed around her.

"I l-l-ove you, Lexiiii. You're my best friend, e-ever!" Cara exclaimed.

"Hey, I thought *I* was your best friend ever?" Fiona whined from behind them.

Cara tried to focus on the voice behind her, failed, and swayed on her feet. "Sure y'aarr, Fi," she shouted, then turned to Lexi, "But I'm reeeeally glad you're going ta be my sisthher, well, sort-a."

Regardless of the hopelessly slurred and contrary words, Lexi experienced a rush of warmth and relief at hearing them. She clung to the hope that Cara's negative attitude had just been the unfounded fears of an insecure sister, rather than a future sister-in-law who hated her guts.

She mentally crossed her fingers. Everything would be fine. She'd probably imagined Cara's disapproval. After all, why else would she offer herself as bridesmaid if she didn't like the idea of her marrying Enzo?

"Love you too, Cara. Now, are you okay to walk, or do you want to sit over there while I fetch the car?" She indicated the bench nearby. Secretly, she hoped they could make it to the car under their own steam. Enzo waited for her. In half an hour, she would be in his arms again. If she hurried.

"I'm fine, fine, fine," Cara sing-songed, then broke into, *"I'm getting married in the morning, tra-la-la-la-la-la-la-la..."*

Relieved, Lexi chuckled as she hooked an arm around her and steered her away from the curb. "You're not getting married for another eight days, love, and the car's this way. Girls, are you all right back there?" she threw over her shoulder at the other two, who propped each other up behind her.

"We're fine, mistress. Lead the way," they chorused.

She smiled. Aside from a few bumps, the evening had gone well. In less than half an hour, it was going to get way better.

She quickened her steps to her car and waited till everyone piled in.

Cara and Fiona were belting their way through a *Cold Play* anthem song when the truck veered across the street and careened straight into their path.

Horns blared.

Someone screamed.

The last thing Lexi saw was the flash of her engagement ring as she threw up her hands in useless defense.

Then the black cloud engulfed her.

Chapter Two

Twelve Months Later

Lexi stepped from the car and sucked in her breath as the hot Los Angeles air stung her nostrils. She still wasn't used to how warm the weather was here compared to the constant wet in London.

In the fading evening light, she looked up at the austere façade of the building in front of her. Pain and sorrow gripped her as it did every time she came here.

Everything remained the same. The sign at the top of the building still read, *St. Jude's Hospital*. The automatic doors she approached would delay in opening until she stood right in front of them, the elevator would creak and groan its way up to the seventh floor, and the smell – the cloying mingled smell of disinfectant and death – would tighten around her throat, as if to strangle her.

Sometimes it took days before the smell came off. It hung around - in her car, her clothes, her hair. Commanding her to never forget.

Never forget.

As if she would.

She touched the inside of her right forearm where the long, thin, jagged scar mocked her. If ever she were in danger of forgetting, she only had to look at her arm to remember. Remember the—

"Hi there, Miss Mayfield. Lord, is it Friday already? The days sure are flying, aren't they?" The buxom black nurse with the salt and pepper hair who worked the evening shift frowned at the calendar on the counter.

"Yes, they are. But it's not Friday. I have to go out of town, so I decided to come a day early." Lexi summoned a smile and approached the desk. "I won't stay long."

"Oh, okay. I thought I was going out of my mind. That, or getting old, which I am, no doubt there. Well, go right on through. There's been no change, unfortunately. But our prayers will be answered one of these days, I'm sure of it." Her smile was benign as she came round the counter and fell into step beside Lexi.

"Thank you."

The older woman laid a hand on her arm. "No, child, don't thank me. I think your devotion has helped a whole lot. The family should be thanking *you*."

You wouldn't say that if you knew. Your smile would turn into a sneer if you only knew the truth. She said nothing. Only nodded and accompanied Nurse Simpson to the last door along the quiet corridor.

She hesitated. When the nurse motioned her inside and departed, Lexi closed the door behind her and approached the bed, the familiar, harrowing, feelings of guilt, sadness and regret, eating away like deadly acid inside her.

Drawing level with the bed, she placed her bag on the floor, pulled up the chair and sat down, never once taking her eyes off the prone form covered with the thin hospital sheet.

She reached out and curled her fingers gently over the open hand resting on the bed.

"Hi, it's Lexi," she whispered as hot tears clouded her eyes.

She'd imagined her tears would've dried up by now, but apparently not. Tears choked her every time she came to the hospital. Some would call it just penance for her sins. But Lexi didn't mind the tears; she welcomed them in fact. At least it showed she was still alive, somewhere deep inside the hollow, numb automaton she had become.

As usual, there was no movement from the bed. The only sounds in the room - the beeping of the heart monitor and the rise and fall of the ventilator - gave what little reassurance it could, that somewhere within the still, pale body on the bed, a spark of life remained.

She sat in silence. She'd given up praying a long time ago. After months of feverishly reciting every prayer she'd ever learned and making up reams of her own, all to no avail, she'd reached the conclusion that prayers were useless. All she could do was be here, infuse what little dregs of hope she had through her touch, her presence.

After what seemed like only a few minutes, she heard voices outside the door. She squinted at her watch and, with a jolt, realized two hours had passed.

Oh God, she couldn't have been here that long! Tension gripped her already stiff shoulders, and she turned toward the door, dread rising as it opened.

At the sight of the figure framed in the doorway, Lexi froze.

Bloody hell.

She'd really hoped to avoid this particular confrontation.

Before she could adjust to the situation or even think up a greeting, the woman approached and snapped, "What the hell are you doing here?"

Lexi folded her hands in her lap. "Same thing you are, I think."

"But it's Thursday. We agreed on the days we would visit. Thursdays are *my* days. So what the fuck are you doing here?" Her so-familiar eyes flashed green fire as she quickly pulled a swathe of shoulder length dark hair to cover the left side of her face.

Lexi's heart twisted at the gesture. "Look, Cara, I don't want any trouble. I'm sorry I encroached on your time. I hadn't intended on staying this long. I only came because I have to go out of town—"

The part of Cara's face she could see contorted in a withering sneer. "Fleeing back to jolly ole England, are you? Leaving us to pick up the pieces you broke our lives into."

"No! I'm not going back to London. I have to go to Vegas for a few days."

The sneer intensified. "It's good for some, isn't it? Today Las Vegas, tomorrow New York, the next Aspen." Cara towered over her and Lexi felt hate wash over her in sickening waves.

"I have to go because it's my job. I'll only be gone for a few days. Next week we can resume our normal routine, and you won't have to see me. I was leaving anyway, so I need not disturb your visit." She gave the hand on the bed one last squeeze and rose.

As she passed her, Cara grabbed her arm in a tight, painful hold, forcing Lexi to stop. "How can you remain so calm? I know you English have that stiff upper lip thing going on, but this is sick. Don't you feel even an ounce of remorse for what you did?"

Dry, shocked laughter escaped Lexi. "How can you say that? Would I be here if I didn't? I tried to talk to you after—after what happened, but you refused to talk to me. If you would just talk to me, Cara—"

Her arm was forcefully thrust away. "I have nothing to say to you. Not after what you did. I told you, I never want to see you again. You make me sick! In the future, if you're going to change the visiting arrangements, inform the nursing staff so they can tell me. Now, get the fuck outta here!" She turned her back on Lexi and walked to the bed.

Lexi picked up her bag, raw pain slicing through her. At the door, she paused. Cara leaned over the bed and took the hand she herself had held for the last two hours. For the sake of her sanity, she decided to give it one last try.

"Cara—"

She rounded on her. "Are you deaf? I told you I have *nothing* to say to you," she spat with enough venom to make Lexi gasp.

Cara turned back to the bed, her voice gentling dramatically. "Fiona, it's Cara. I'm here, sweetheart. I've come to see you."

***

Lexi choked back her sobs and stumbled out the door. The pale hospital walls receded as memories crashed through her head like giant waves.

Twelve months. Or to be exact, eleven months, three weeks and one day, since the crash that had ripped four lives and families apart.

She tore down the hall, the echo of her heels taking her back…back…

London...the night of the bachelorette party…four giggling women getting into Lexi's Beetle…Lexi secretly pleased they all lived relatively close together so she could drop them all off and still make it to Enzo's house within the half hour.

Was that why she'd been going a tad over the speed limit? Probably.

All she knew was that none of them had made it home that night.

The last thing she remembered was turning into the road leading to the apartment Cara shared with Ian, her panic at the blinding lights of the truck that loomed out of nowhere…on the wrong side of the road… She remembered the screams, the horrible screams, before everything turned black.

She'd come out of a hazy fog by the roadside, propped up on the ambulance gurney. The policeman instructed her to blow into the Breathalyzer. Numbly, she'd complied, all the while staring with displaced horror at the remains of what used to be her car.

The rear had completely disappeared, the front seats held together by a precarious tangle of metal. She'd watched a tow truck lift the twisted heap onto its platform with a detached sense of shock.

But as it'd driven past her, and she'd spied Fiona's diamante-studded right shoe dangling from the mangled pile, she'd lost it, her hysterical screams ripping through the converged crowd. She'd felt a pinprick in her arm, before everything had once again gone mercifully blank.

She'd woken up in the hospital, her right arm in a tight bandage, and her left wrist handcuffed to the bed, while a policeman stood guard at the foot of her bed.

He'd instructed her to blow into a similar gadget as the Breathalyzer and calmly informed her that Sally was dead.

She'd died instantly, having taken the major brunt of the collision to the rear left hand side of the car. Fiona, who'd been beside Sally, was in surgery fighting for her life. Cara, although she'd suffered head injuries, was out of immediate danger, but in intensive care.

As for her, by some freak of nature, she'd escaped with nothing more than minor injuries to the right arm she'd thrown up to cover her face as the windshield glass shattered. The drunk driver of the truck had also escaped injury.

She'd been released three hours later after a severe grilling from the policeman who'd taken her statement and ordered her to report to the station the next day. Her request to see her friends had been denied, what with Fiona still in surgery and Cara allowed only one visitor, her brother, for the moment.

Fleetingly, as she absorbed news of Sally's death, she'd wondered why Enzo hadn't come to see her. She'd berated herself. At that moment, his sister needed him more than she did. She'd see him the next day when the dust had cleared a little. But it'd still hurt that he hadn't come to find out how she was.

As it'd turned out, fate had other plans for her. Technically and lawfully, the accident had been the fault of the truck driver, but she'd known she was also to blame, that she'd never be free of it. If she hadn't taken that fiery swig of the cosmo, hadn't been in such a hurry to drop the girls off and see Enzo, things would've been different. And for that mistake, Fate demanded she serve a life sentence for *one* moment of foolishness.

Mired in the darkest moments of her past, Lexi staggered out into the early evening air. A small eddy of dust blew past and brought her back to the present. She stopped on the sidewalk, blinked back her tears, and clenched her hands to stop their trembling. The wind whipped her hair over her face, and she caught the smell - the dreaded hospital scent - in her nostrils.

Jump-started by the stench, she tore through her handbag, frantic in her hunt for her keys. Grabbing them, she ran to her car, yanked open the door and threw her bag on the passenger seat.

She'd just twisted the key in the ignition when a hand rapped on the window.

Startled, she glanced up and found Cara next to her car, hatred still simmering in her green eyes. With apprehension, Lexi lowered her window.

"I came to remind you of your other promise. Just in case you've forgotten it like you forgot what day it was today."

Almost immediately, guilt churned in Lexi's stomach. Guilt and resentment for what Cara had made her promise six months ago when she'd arrived in LA.

A promise she'd had no business demanding of her. And one Lexi shouldn't have sworn to keep.

Her shoulders slumped with the weight of her disappointment.

She'd hoped Cara had come after her for something else. Like a willingness to listen to Lexi's part in what had happened. But no. She'd come to twist the knife further.

"I haven't forgotten Cara. Believe me, I haven't forgotten anything," she replied. Then drove away.

***

Lexi let herself into her sixth floor condo in downtown Santa Monica, grateful for its cool serenity. Her bag landed on the polished hardwood floor. She lobbed her keys onto the nearby coffee table, and headed straight for her bedroom, removing her wraparound dress as she went. She needed a shower like she needed her next breath. Three-inch heels came off next to the case she'd packed for her trip to Vegas in the morning. Lexi paused long enough to slip out of her panties and bra.

The scalding shower was a welcome, cleansing relief, turned on full blast in the hopes of scouring away the turmoil within. She lathered more shampoo than was necessary into her hair, scrubbed vigorously until her scalp tingled, then repeated the process twice, before finally turning the water to tepid and then cool. After switching it off, she wrapped herself in a large, fluffy towel.

Tying another smaller towel around her head, she re-entered her bedroom and paused when her gaze landed on the cards on her dresser.

The big 3-0 had arrived last month and, save a couple of well-wishing cards and calls from one or two friends in London and her grandmother in Edinburgh, she'd passed the day alone in her condo, by herself, with Chinese take-out and a can of soda. She'd refused the free bottle of wine from the delivery guy, who announced cheerfully that it came compliments of the house, seeing as it had been her twentieth order.

He'd been taken aback by her refusal. After all, who refused a freebie, even if it was cheap plonk?

How was he to know she didn't drink anymore? That not a single drop of alcohol had passed her lips in almost a year? How could he tell that the woman who ordered *Kung Pow* chicken and shredded beef noodles every Wednesday night without fail now lived her life by a series of vows? The very first being that, for Fiona's sake, for Cara's, but most of all for Sally's precious memory, she'd vowed to spend the rest of her life sober, seeing everything in crystal clarity, lest another stupid alcohol-fuelled decision wrecked another life.

Sally. Oh God, Sally! Hot tears filled her eyes and she sank onto her bed. Saying goodbye to her childhood friend had been one of the hardest things Lexi had ever done. A double blow, considering she'd been banned from Sally's funeral by her parents, who laid the blame for their daughter's death squarely at Lexi's feet. They'd even refused to speak to her after discovering from the police report how close she'd been to the drink-driving limit. She shuddered as she recalled Sally's father thick, pain-filled rant that *she* should have died, not his daughter.

On the day of Sally's funeral, she'd waited in her car for hours, just to be sure everyone had left before going to her friend's graveside. There she'd said goodbye, and made her vow never to touch another drop of liquor for as long as she lived. So far she'd kept that promise. That particular promise had been easy to keep.

As for the other promise, the one Cara had reminded her of half an hour ago…

Lexi shook her head, shut off the thoughts and dashed away her tears. Her diary lay on her bedside table. She picked it up and opened it to the date she'd marked with a triple X. Snatching up her phone, she placed the call to double-check the flowers she'd ordered to be delivered to Sally's grave in the London suburb they'd grown up in. Then she ordered the same to be delivered to Fiona's room. Fresh wisteria, to drive away the sharp smell of disinfectant.

Although the anniversary of the accident fell next Friday, one of her visiting days, she aimed to stay away. Fiona's parents, and Cara most likely, would want to spend all day with her. And the last thing she wanted was another confrontation with Cara.

She released the knot on the towel and dropped it on the floor. Naked, she walked into her closet, reached for her blue velour joggers and stopped as she heard the beep of her smart phone.

Throwing the clothes on the bed, she returned to the living room, fetched the phone, and activated it.

Blood surged through her veins when she recognized the number. The message itself was simple.

Vegas?

Ah, news traveled fast.

She answered. *Yes. Work.*

Meet me tonight.

She swallowed. *It's Thursday.*

Meet me. Same time. Same place.

Fingers poised over the keys, she sank onto the nearest chair, raw indecision eating at her. She needed this. Tonight of all nights, she needed this so badly. Her thumb moved, then froze as Cara's warning echoed in her head.

Dammit. R u there?

Yes, I'm here, she responded. Where else would she be?

You have one hour. And don't even think about not showing up.

God help her. She needed this.

I'll be there.

Her whole body trembling, she shoved the phone back into her bag and returned to the bedroom. Stark naked, clothes forgotten, she laid back on her bed, staring at the ceiling.

She'd broken her promise. The only one she couldn't keep. Again.

It didn't matter that she'd kept half of the whole promise; breaking even a small part of it always left a hollow feeling of guilt inside her.

But to honor the promise would mean giving up the one small part of her life that kept her sane.

I need this.

She closed her eyes, already transported to the future, an hour away. The heated slide of hands, the skilful thrust of tongues, the potent smell of aroused bodies, and the electrifying pleasure-pain of a stiff cock pushing inside her – hard on soft.

And yes, the monumental guilt that always followed, ready to consume, to annihilate.

Six months, she'd lived with it. She would continue to live with it, until something gave. As she had no doubt it would.

***

Just over an hour later, she parked in the underground car park of an apartment complex in an affluent neighborhood in West Hollywood, entered the private elevator, and pressed the button for the penthouse suite. She snatched a shaky breath, smoothed clammy hands down her red leather skirt, and watched the doors slide shut. Somehow, even the guilt made the anticipation sharper, sweeter. Like a child playing hooky for the first time, thoughts of discovery always lurked, but alongside was the hope that maybe, just maybe, she might get away with it.

The elevator climbed higher, along with her excitement. Her lace-covered nipples hardened into throbbing peaks and pushed against her bra; the warm rush of air against her naked thighs caused goose flesh to break out all over her skin.

She'd worn her freshly dried hair up, a futile exercise, since it'd be freed from its knot the minute she walked in the door. But it was all just part of the sequence of events. Things had to happen a certain way, always.

Her skirt had to be short, her top easily removable; her lips had to be tinged with the slightest of gloss, but her fingers and toes painted a fiery red. The "no underwear" clause she'd firmly vetoed, not because of propriety, but because she loved the sensual feel of the material as it slid off her skin. Or when it was tugged firmly between her butt cheeks, creating a sweet friction on her clit. More often than not though, it was more of a ripping and less of a sliding.

Her lips parted on a soft exhalation as the elevator pinged its arrival.

The door opposite, bland and unprepossessing, cleverly masked what lay within. She approached, used her key, and let herself in.

The large sunken living room, decorated in minimalist black and white, was empty. Soft lights played on chrome and glass tables and lent a deceptive calm to the room. On one side, facing two large sofas, floor to ceiling windows reflected the soft lighting as well as the spectacular vista of LA at night. On the other side of the room, set against the back wall, a long bar, complete with elegant ladder-back stools, held pride of place.

Turning away from the view, she walked to the bar, poured herself a large mineral water, and took a long drink. It would be hours before she came up for air, water or sustenance of any kind, she mused.

The empty glass discarded on the counter-top, she made sure her cell phone was switched off, left her small evening bag next to it, and slowly turned toward the short hallway.

She barely noticed the expensive abstract paintings on the walls. Her eyes remained riveted on the gleaming black door at the end of the corridor.

Dark excitement ratcheted up another thousand notches. The tips of her fingers tingled in anticipation of turning the knob; her blood roared through her veins. An addict seeking her next fix. That's what she felt like. And it would be sweet, so, so sweet.

She reached for the door handle, tongue sneaking out to coat her dry lips, and turned it.

And there, on the bed, in blue jeans, white T-shirt, and black leather jacket, sat her guilt, her pleasure, her pain.

"Hello, Enzo."

Chapter Three

Lorenzo Saldana watched Lexi walk toward him, struck dumb all over again by her stunning beauty. For some reason, the sight of her, looking even more beautiful than she had just a week ago, made his simmering anger rise.

Her peach-perfect skin glowed in the soft lamplight. Her silky hair was up, secured with a clip of some sort, but already a few strands fought the restraint. The loose wisps caressed her smooth cheeks and delicate jaw. His fingers itched to release the rest of the glorious chocolate brown mass and feel it slide over his hand, his arms. The need to wind it round his fist, use it to tilt her face up to his, and taste her sinful, delicious mouth burned like an inferno through him. But he stayed put, hands fisted on his thighs.

Over the thunder-strong beat of his heart, he heard her soft, short breathing and knew she was just as excited as he. The hard-on he'd sported for longer than he cared to think about grew thicker and strained against his jeans. She'd taken her time walking through the apartment; dragged out the moment before she entered the bedroom. Each second he'd waited had made his blood surge higher, his pulse race faster.

But he didn't mind the anticipation, however fucking excruciating.

It was all part of the game. An elaborate foreplay - *the song and dance* - as she called it.

He resisted the urge to grab her, tear off her clothes, ram deep inside her hot, tight wetness – and oh, he knew she'd be wet. Wet and ready.

No, for now he'd play along. The reward would be all the sweeter for the wait, the patience. His lips twitched as he recalled a scene from the Japanese comic books he'd devoured as a kid. The grand master always instructed his pupil to practice fortitude – *never go with your first instinct to react.* Yeah, patience is a fucking virtue...

So he waited.

She took another step, nudging the door shut behind her. Her long, sexy legs made him imagine them slung over his shoulders, urging him deeper as he thrust into her slick, greedy cunt. She stopped in front of him, her slim arms loose at her sides.

"Hello, Enzo," she repeated, gazing down at him. No smile curved her lips, no happiness reflected in her eyes. Only the naked sheen of want and the hot scent of sex.

She craved him as much as he craved her, there'd never been any doubt about *that*. Everything else had gotten messed up badly but the insane, visceral need to fuck each other's brains out whenever they were within eye-catching distance of one another had never been in dispute, or had it ever diminished.

Several times in the past he'd doubted the power of that need.

Time and again he'd been proved wrong. Lexi Mayfield was the potent drug he'd never got the cure for…hell he wasn't sure he ever wanted to be cured of this addiction. Even in his darkest hours, when he let himself remember how much her betrayal had burned, he still wanted her with a ferocity that made him doubt his sanity.

It was that insanity that had driven him here today – a day outside of their prearranged schedule. Not that he cared much. His need was too damned strong to deny.

Breathing out again, he watched her, followed the lines of the exquisite hour-glass figure that would soon be his to possess once again.

"Aren't you going to respond, Enzo?" she asked.

Silhouetted against the soft material of her black top, her nipples had peaked into hard points. Desire watered his mouth, both at the look in her eyes and the way her sexy British accent clipped his name out. It was in direct contrast to the way she sounded when he was deep inside her, fucking her to near delirium. Then, his name sounded soft and breathless.

He tamped down the need to make that happen immediately. Not yet…

"Hey, baby. I was beginning to think you wouldn't show."

Her eyes remained on him, restlessly devouring him. "I hit a bit of traffic."

He nodded, then he asked the crucial question that had burned a hole in his mind ever since he found out she was going out of town.

"How long will you be in Vegas?"

If the question surprised her, she didn't show it. Her spiky-lashed blue gaze remained on him, her body hummed, awaiting his touch. "Five days," she breathed, as the tip of her tongue snuck out and quickly disappeared back in again.

Unwanted relief poured through him. Five days – he could live with that. But that wasn't what annoyed him. "Were you going to tell me you'd be out of town?"

"I didn't see the need. It's not like it would affect our arrangement."

"That's not the point. I shouldn't have to find out you're going out of town from someone else."

That someone else being his sister, who'd relished delivering the message.

His jaw clenched. She saw and her eyes darkened. "Are we really going to do this now, Enzo? Waste time when I have to be at the airport in a few hours? I'll be back before you get a chance to miss me." She gave a hollow laugh. Because missing each other meant they cared.

And *caring* wasn't what this was about. It had been once upon a time. When he'd foolishly invested his whole future in her.

No. This time round, it was all about the sex. Soul searing, sheet ripping sex that left him reeling for days. The kind of sex that made him slightly nuts at the thought of her going out of state and being out of reach. Theirs may be a weekly tryst but he felt soothed knowing she was in the same city.

"As long as you promise there won't be a repeat of what happened when you were in Aspen, we'll be okay."

"I don't think snow is forecast for Vegas this week."

"It had better not be. I want you back here in five days, or I'm coming to get you wherever the hell you are."

Aspen. Only hellishly cold showers and the impossibility of removing himself from his sister's clutches on short notice had stopped him hopping on a plane and tracking her down at her hotel when she'd been stuck there two months ago. On the bright side, he'd known once and for all then that he wasn't suffering this insanity alone. He'd stayed put in LA, and his patience had paid dividends.

She'd returned, crazy hot for him, wearing a tight skirt that had made him want to hunt down and kill every man who'd seen her sexy little ass.

He'd brought her here straight from the airport, and they'd barely walked in the door before she'd ripped his clothes off, almost sobbing with need.

"Fuck me, please. Fuck me now!" she'd begged.

He'd rammed into her, right there, up against the front door. Shit, he'd never come so quickly in his life. Luckily, she'd come just as fast, her hoarse screams echoing through the apartment.

He loved her screams. Especially the way she threw her head back just before she let them rip. That particular experience still had the power to blow his mind. The lack of foreplay, the rough and readiness of it, the crazed possession of each other. His cock threatened to explode just thinking of it.

So why not now?

Take her and to hell with foreplay.

"You don't own me, Enzo. So stop growling out threats. If I have to stay longer in Vegas it would be because of work, and I won't have you jeopardizing that under any circumstances. Right now it's the only important thing in my life." Pain darkened her eyes and a bite of regret cut through his supremely aroused state.

Yeah, there was a lot of pain and regret all round. He could forgive a lot of things, but never betrayal. And hers had been the ultimate betrayal.

He reached a hand up, curled it over her hip, clasped his other on the back of her neck and forced her head down. She gasped and braced her hands on his shoulders to keep her balance.

"You think I don't own you? Then what are you doing here? From the moment I saw you, you've been mine. You've fucked up a beautiful thing beyond reason, but you still belong to me."

"No, I came because I wanted to. It was my choice, my free will."

"Bullshit. You're trembling with the promise of what I am about to do to you. You crave me, you exist for this. Nothing and no one can come close to giving you what I can, not even your precious job. *You came because you belong to me*. It's as simple as that. I call, you come."

"On Fridays. I belong to you only on *Fridays*," she whispered. "And I didn't fuck us up, Enzo. I know you don't believe me—"

He dragged her down and shut her up with a kiss. Firstly because he didn't want to be reminded of the past, but mostly because he'd had enough of *the song and dance*.

The need to kiss her trumped all else.

At the first taste of her, his anger receded. She was hot, potent, pure temptation. And her smell – an alluring blend of summer sunshine, apples, and orgiastic sex - made his chest tighten with lust and pain. Everything he'd missed like crazy in the past six days was within his arms. Everything she would've denied him if his sister hadn't called him, furious at Lexi's unscheduled appearance at the hospital.

If he hadn't contacted Lexi, she'd have left for Vegas without a word, without fulfilling her weekly bargain to him. His anger returned with a vengeance. Wrenching his mouth from her clinging lips, he pushed her away and sat back.

"Take off your clothes," he instructed.

Confusion clouded her eyes. "What?"

Normally, that was his job, a task he took much pleasure in performing. But not today.

"Take. Off. Your. Clothes."

Wild excitement fleeted across her eyes, but her confusion remained.

She planted her hands on her hips. "Don't you want to do it?" she asked, her slightly pointed chin tilted in challenge.

"Not tonight."

Her fingers caressed subtly over her skirt, drawing his gaze to the waist he knew his hands could span.

"I'm wearing your favorite color," she whispered, taking a half step toward him, a small smile teasing over her lips, gone as quickly as it arrived.

"I can see." His eyes drifted down over the red skirt, red nail polish, and the red platform stilettos. He wondered if the red was repeated underneath. God, he hoped so. His pulse hammered. "Show me," he commanded, fighting the urge to grab the collar of her top, ripping it open to see for himself.

Rising, he moved away from her, taking himself, for the moment, out of temptation's way. He pulled the stack of condoms from his back pocket and dropped them on the bedside table. His jacket and shoes came off next and he settled himself in the middle of the bed. Better keep the rest of his clothes on for now. He dragged in a deep breath to relax his throbbing body. An impossibility, with his rock hard cock shooting urgent "I wanna fuck" messages to his brain.

"Come on, baby, step it up, would you? I'm hard for you. Harder than I've ever been and you don't want this to go to waste, do you?" He pointed to his bulging trousers and watched her gaze drop to his crotch. At the evidence of his ungodly erection, a moan escaped her lips. "That's right, this is all for you. Take your clothes off and come and get it," he encouraged softly. "That's why we're both here, isn't it?" He ran a hand over his erection and almost caused himself a coronary. A silent curse ripped through his mind.

What the hell was he doing, taunting them both like this? At this rate, he would pass out before he got the chance to put a finger on her. He watched her and hid his sigh of relief when she hurried out of her black suede coat and dropped it to the floor.

Then she reached up behind her, one hand wriggling up her back to reach the zipper on her high collared top. The gentleman in him wanted to help, but he curbed the instinct, enjoying her little contortions and the play of her full breasts as her chest heaved with her efforts. It was almost a shame when she got the zipper down. But when she peeled the top up over her head, he remembered - payback was a bitch.

Her breasts almost spilled out of demi cups of blood red lace, while the barest hint of dusky pink aureolas peeked over of the top. God, they were perfect, so fucking perfect, he swallowed a moan. His stomach clenched and the hand next to his thigh fisted on the bed.

Jesus, would he ever stop wanting this woman? What was it about her that fired up his blood to volcanic levels?

The top joined the jacket on the floor. She stepped out of the skirt, and then he knew. Her face might be one of an angel's, but her body would've driven even Botticelli mad with desire. Perfectly shaped and expertly formed, the amazing dips and curves made his mouth literally water with yearning. He stared, eyes riveted on the shadow between her thighs, as desire pulse through him.

His tongue craved to taste her, *right there*.

"Come here," he rasped, not caring that his voice came out a dark croak.

She looked at him from beneath sooty lashes. "I'm still wearing my shoes." She gestured to them with a fluttery, feminine movement, contrived or unconscious on her part, he wasn't sure, but designed to drive a man wild. It worked. Her helplessness made him even harder.

"Leave them on," he ordered again.

"Are...are you sure?" Once again, confusion gleamed in her eyes.

"More than," he rasped. "Tonight, we're changing things up a bit. Don't worry, you'll love it. Now, come here."

She swallowed and her eyes flickered over him once more.

He kept his gaze on her as she walked slowly round the bed to stand next to him. Raising his hand, he ran a finger down the side of her thigh and reveled in the shudder that shook her frame. It was good to know she experienced the same crazed reaction he felt when they touched. It eased the lust-engorged monster raging within him.

She lifted her hand, no doubt to touch him in return, but he stopped her with a look.

"Take off your panties before I rip them off. Leave the bra and shoes on."

As her trembling hands moved to do his bidding, her eyes darted to his crotch and back to his face, her hunger stark and raw. He smiled and shook his head, denying her what she most craved. With the back of his hand, he caressed the exposed dark curls between her legs. She jerked and tried to move closer. He removed his hand and levered himself up against the pillows.

"Enzo," she whispered in heated desire.

He heard the pleading in her voice and steeled himself against it. Tonight they would do things *his way*.

He held out a hand to her. "Climb up on the bed, one foot on either side of me. Careful with those heels," he joked, casting her a taut smile. "I don't want a punctured lung to put a dampener on things."

After a moment's hesitation, she put her hand in his and climbed onto the bed. He held onto her, helping her maintain her balance until she was steady. He released her and she braced both hands on the wall behind the bed.

From this position, the sight above him made his heart slam so hard inside his chest, he seriously feared for his health. But it wasn't enough. He wanted more.

"Good, now, come closer."

She moved up a step.

"Closer."

"Enzo," her voice was now a confused protest.

"*Do it*."

She moved until her feet were planted on either side of his shoulders. He looked up. And groaned. Nestled between her perfect legs, he spied the twin lips of her labia, moist and ready for him. Further up, past the dark curls, the soft curve of her stomach gave way to a flat midriff, above which surged the perfect globes of her lace-cupped breasts.

But something was missing. *Something…*

"Release your hair," he grated and gave in to the urge to touch, to run his hands from her ankles to her calves. Her warm, silky smooth skin felt like velvet. He couldn't stop himself from caressing for a few more seconds, while he watched her posed above him.

Glorious. She was just...glorious.

She closed her eyes briefly, her breath choppy. Then she reached behind her head and pulled out the clip. The chocolate river spilled around her bent head, framing her face and teasing her shoulders and breasts. *Perfect.*

"Now, here's what I want you to do," he rasped. "Slowly sink down and give me a taste of that sweet, juicy cunt."

***

Lexi moaned again, certain any second now she'd lose her mind. Her whole body trembled and her heart was racing so fast, it could've won the London Marathon a dozen times already.

Looking down into Enzo's smoky green eyes, she tried to read the expression in them. Fierce desire, relentless hunger...and simmering anger. But that was nothing new. He hated himself and her for the power of their attraction as much as she hated herself for the very same reason.

But something had changed tonight. Where they'd shared equal power in what happened in this bedroom every Friday night, tonight he seemed to be calling all the shots.

And she was letting him.

Why?

Had the events of the day sapped what little willpower she had left? Or had she been waiting all along for a moment like this, to relinquish the power to him? Her thoughts fled when he reached higher and trailed both hands up the inside of her thighs.

"I'm ready and waiting, baby, come to me," he urged in his husky, dark voice.

Another tremor went through her. Anticipation of what would happen once she bent her knees the way he wished almost robbed her of breath. He'd given her oral pleasure before, but never like this. This was…raw, elemental and almost demeaning.

But she was also beyond excited. So much so she feared it would kill her.

Bracing her hand on the wall, she sank down a few inches.

"Come on," he crooned. "It'll be good, I promise."

She sank further and felt the strain in her quivering thighs.

"I'm waiting."

She almost said, *I'm coming*, and the thought nearly made her smile. No doubt there. She could already feel the telltale signs shooting through her body.

The farther down she went, the more he supported her. And the more she exposed herself to his fiery, devouring gaze. She saw his eyes widen slightly, his nostrils flare and his full mouth pucker ever so faintly as his hands tightened on her.

"Do you like what you see, Enzo?" she asked, not yet willing to relinquish all the power.

His gaze darted from where it'd been riveted between her legs to her face. A hard grin lit his olive toned features, but it did nothing to diminish the fire in his eyes.

"You have the most beautiful cunt I've ever seen. Like the palest pink petals of a flower washed in morning dew. In a second I'm going to taste you, and then I'll tell you what morning dew tastes like," he replied, exerting pressure on her thighs.

Lexi shuddered, almost afraid to go all the way. But Enzo's strong hands on her thighs propelled her down, and there was only one way to go.

Another few inches, and she saw his lips part, his tongue sneak out to rest against his lower lip. Oh, dear God. The spasms in her pelvis intensified.

Enzo groaned, shifting restlessly beneath her as anticipation burned them both.

Then with a final twist, he reversed his arms, hooked his hands under her thighs, and pulled her down the rest of the way, lifting his head to his prize.

At the first pass of his tongue over her clit, she came. Wildly, helplessly, head back, she thrashed violently on top of him.

"Oh God! *Omigod!*" She screamed as sensation buffeted her.

By some miracle, he kept her in place, his mouth never once leaving her pulsing flesh. Lexi's orgasm went on forever and her screams bounced off the walls. And through it all, he laved her with his tongue, licking and sucking on ultra-sensitive tissue. He drank her up, groaning appreciatively, deep and long, as she gushed in his mouth. The hands she'd braced against the wall slipped. She lowered them to grip the carved headboard as spasms continued to wrack her.

In some distant part of her brain, she registered that she was fucking his face, her hips moving of their own accord as residual convulsions pulsed through her. The thought almost made her come again. When he angled his head and his stubble brushed roughly against her inner thighs, she let out another cry and held on for dear life as tears of bliss burned behind her closed lids.

Finally, with a last lick, Enzo lowered his head onto the pillow and looked up at her. "Ambrosia, baby. The very best kind," he said, satisfaction coating his voice.

Lexi struggled to make out the meaning of his words, and failed. "What?"

"You taste of the sweetest ambrosia. Heavenly, addictive, and totally mind-blowing."

The sight of his lips coated with her come almost flipped her mind. "Can I taste it too?"

His eyes darkened from jade to moss. Repositioning her onto her knees, he slowly flicked one finger over her engorged clit, then slid it inside her. She groaned, her muscles clenching greedily around him. He stayed there for a moment, his other hand coming up to palm one breast. Blood surged higher and her moan turned into a keen.

"Enzo, please," she begged. With one hand, she reached behind her, stroking his erection, need clamoring through her once more.

"I thought you wanted a taste of heaven?" he queried softly.

"Yes, yes, I want…I want that too."

"Hmm, greedy aren't you?" he teased, laughing softly. "Come here." Trailing his hand from her breast to the back of her neck, he pulled her down, at the same time removing his finger from her trembling core. He brought her closer until they were centimeters apart and held up his finger between them. "Let's taste paradise together," he rasped.

She swooped the rest of the way, her tongue lapping the moisture on his finger, moaning as his own tongue came out to join with hers. Together they licked every last drop, then, his finger abandoned, they kissed with a wildness bordering on the crazed, cocooned within the curtain of her hair.

Lexi ran her hands over his shoulders, finally seizing the freedom to touch him. Encountering soft cotton, she protested, slid her hands down until she touched the hot skin of his washboard stomach. His muscles clenched at her touch, his immediate reaction causing her to moan again. He swallowed her moan as his tongue dueled fiercely with hers. Sensation gripped her, her inner muscles twitching with the urgent need to fuck him.

Tearing her lips from his, she traced her mouth along his jaw, and rubbed herself against the rough stubble that had moment ago grazed her thighs. She caught the faint, musky smell of her orgasm on his skin and her whole body tightened with pleasure.

God, she loved that smell. It may have been irrational but she loved to brand him with her scent, to know that for a few hours, in this time and space, he was hers.

His hands trailed down her back, gliding hot against her skin to her butt. Curving his big hands around her ass, he squeezed her flesh before coming up again. When he encountered her bra, he yanked it off, and cupped both breasts in his hands.

He sighed with satisfaction. "Glorious." He caressed them and grazed his thumbs across the aroused peaks. Just when she thought she'd go out of her mind, he raised his head and took one nub in his mouth.

"Oh yes," she gasped, eyes shut to absorb the sensation. With his other hand, he continued to work on her breast. Her pussy moistened again, hot liquid rushing out of her. She needed to fuck him, right now, or she'd die.

"Enzo, I need you. Please..." She looked down at him, at his mouth on her nipple, at the harsh beauty of the man beneath her.

He paused.

"Please what?" The question was a hot breath against her flesh, turning her on harder.

"Please, let me fuck you."

He rested his head against the pillows, his gaze on hers as he continued to lick her nipple. A hard smile crossed his face.

"So you want this? And yet you were going to leave without coming to get it. Why should I let you have it now?"

"I...I wasn't thinking straight." As usual, Cara had succeeded in arousing her guilt, reminded her of the lives she'd ruined. So much so, she'd almost denied herself *this*. "I'm sorry."

"And are you going to fix it? Are you going to use that tight little cunt to fuck me better?"

"Yes. God, yes." Her need was almost out of control. Lexi shook with the thought of having him inside her.

"Guess what, baby," he crooned, "I'm going to let you."

He yanked off his T-shirt over his head and threw it on the floor.

Like a child given permission to play with a new toy, she fell on his exposed torso, licking and sucking flat male nipples into hardened nubs, before heading due south of his golden flesh to the waistband of his jeans. She nipped the glorious skin below his navel, popped the button, and lowered his zipper, enjoying his feral growl when she raked urgent hands down his body. He buried his hands in her hair as she tugged his trousers down, taking his boxers with it. A soft sigh escaped her as his enormous, thickly veined cock strained toward her, its tip already wet with sweet nectar.

In happier times, before tragedy had ripped their lives apart, she'd composed adoring odes to his *delectable shag-*

shaft. Now, all she wanted was to take it in her mouth and feel its velvety length all the way to the back of her throat.

Running her hands up his inner thighs, she cupped his balls in one hand, felt the soft silky flesh tighten in immediate response, while her other hand gripped his cock and closed her lips round it. She moaned. He groaned. Her pussy clenched in greedy anticipation as she sucked him deeper. When her tongue flicked in urgent licks across his head, his hands tightened in her hair.

"You don't want to do that, baby. I'm extremely close to the edge right now and I want this to be a helluva lot more than a five-minute ride," he warned tersely.

Five minutes, hell five *seconds* would suit her just fine, she wagered. But when his hands gripped firmly in her hair, she knew she'd have to wait a little longer to taste his essence in her mouth. Reluctantly, she curled her tongue round him a last time, then turned her attention to licking his balls while he ripped open a condom.

He'd barely glided it on before she'd repositioned herself on top of him. With a deep sigh, she sank down. Hot fire shot through her as her flesh stretched almost painfully to accommodate him.

Holding her still, he pushed just a little deeper.

She winced and cried out. He stopped immediately.

"Fuck! I don't know why I always forget just how fucking tight you are," he growled through gritted teeth. "I'm sorry, baby."

She shook her head. "Don't be. I love how you stretch me."

Relief poured over his face. "Yeah?" Tentatively, he pulled out and slid back in.

"Oh God, yes. Your cock feels so good inside me," she gasped. A little more accustomed to him, she rocked back and forth, relearning the feel of him, the very many ways he could make this experience even more mind-blowing.

Before she'd taken a few breaths, Enzo had established a spine-tingling rhythm, one guaranteed to drive her right out of her mind.

Unwilling to let go just yet, Lexi's hands slid up his chest, greedy to feel all of him.

His hands flexed on her ass, pressing her down further on top of him, until they were pussy to crotch. "But I bet not as good as you feel around me," he growled, encouraging her rocking motion.

She leaned forward to run her tongue over his mouth, and sank back down. Up and down she rode, heady with the pressure that rose in her pelvis.

The rhythm increased, their mingled breaths turning harsh as they locked themselves into a frenzied dance. Just when she thought she'd hit her pinnacle, Enzo paused, rearranged her so her feet were planted on either side of his waist and her hands gripped his thighs behind her. With his hands on her ass, he raised her up and brought her down hard on top of him.

"Jesus," she cried, the sensation of being ripped apart causing explosions in her brain.

"Feel good?"

She was beyond words, but she rose up and repeated the action. Again. And again. Locked into an even more mind-blowing rhythm, she rode him hard, head thrown back, hoarse cries accompanying every thrust. Beneath her, Enzo's throaty groans mirrored hers as they neared orgasm.

"Come on, baby," he urged, a tense note in his voice. "Come on, give me that sweet ambrosia again. Squeeze me; that's it, again! Jesus, you look so fucking hot like that. Fuck, yeah! Take it baby, take it all." One finger found her clit, teased the wet nub, sent her higher and higher.

The storm beckoned, rushed toward her with lightning speed. Sensation raced over her, drowned her in heat and bliss that made her whole body shudder.

"Oh my God, Enzo, I'm coming!"

"Fuck, I hope so, 'cuz so am I!" came his hoarse warning. A second later, she splintered, jerking wildly with the force of her climax. Beneath her, he pumped once, twice, then he stilled. "I'm gonna come so hard for you, baby. So. Damned. Hard."

The cords in his neck tightened, his jaw clenching as his fingers dug painfully into her ass.

He gave a hoarse shout as he lost it, urged on by her contracting inner muscles. His finger stayed pressed against her clit, forcing a longer release as she continued to shudder on top of him, her cries of pleasure once again echoing off the walls.

After several minutes, she calmed. With a tug from him, she collapsed onto his chest, boneless, sated.

He ran callused hands up and down her back and over her flanks until their harsh breaths eased, before shifting her onto the bed. Then he rose and headed for the adjoining bathroom.

Lexi watched Enzo go, unable to resist the sight of his mouth-watering body. He had the V-shaped, deep-chested torso of a gladiator, a firm ass, powerful thighs and hard muscled legs to match the rest of his toned body.

The large tattoo of an eagle soaring between his shoulder blades just added to his overall, mouthwatering appeal. His shoulder-length black hair had been one of the things that had turned her on first time she'd met him. When she told him so, he'd cocked a smile, and said, "Yeah, I get that a lot."

Memories of that first time and the heady days that had followed threatened to crash in, but she pushed them away. This wasn't the time or the place. The running water shut off and a second later, Enzo re-entered the room. His powerful presence filled the space, and the eyes that immediately zeroed in on her caused her skin to prickle with renewed awareness.

He approached the bed, his semi-hard cock swinging against his thigh. Fresh need clawed through her.

God, how was that even possible? She'd come twice in the last twenty minutes, yet she ached for his cock again.

Her scrutiny was having an effect on him as well, and she watched, fascinated, as his erection grew, slowly rising from its nest of black curls until it strained, thick and heavy, toward her. Moaning, she rose from the bed, and crawled on her knees to him. He stopped at the side of the bed and looked down at her. Slowly, he leaned forward and took her mouth in a long, hot kiss. After several minutes, he let her up for air and leaned his forehead against hers.

"I'm dying to fuck you again, but I don't want to make you sore."

"I can think of other ways to while away the time..." She slowly circled her tongue over his lips, then leaned back and glanced down meaningfully.

He straightened and sank his hands into her hair, nostrils flaring as he inhaled sharply and nodded.

"Do you want it fast or slow?"

He gave an agonized groan. "I'll take it anyway you give it to me, baby," he rasped.

"Hmm...okay."

Gripping him in one hand, she flicked her tongue over his velvet-smooth cock, enjoying the salty, musky taste of him. Licking her way down his rigid length, she followed the thick vein back up again, before swirling her tongue over his silken head. He opened his legs wider and thrust his hips forward. She took him deeper into her mouth, sliding down on him until he hit the back of her throat.

His breath hissed through his teeth. "Fuck, that feels so good. *Jesus.*"

A quick glance up showed his head thrown back, eyes closed, and his mouth open on oxygen-sucking gasps. She curved her tongue around him and increased the pressure of her mouth as she stroked him up and down. One hand left her hair and came around to palm a breast. He squeezed and tweaked her nipple. She jerked, involuntary spasms gripping her. The pressure on her nipples increased.

"You like that, baby?" he croaked.

"Hmm," she moaned.

"How about this?" He slid his other hand down her back until he reached the crack in her ass. Gliding down further through her wetness, he inserted two fingers deep inside her wet pussy.

"Ahh," she moaned again, releasing him with an eager gasp, "Yes," before going back to her delicious task. She turned to give him better access, wriggling her butt against his hand, eager for him to finger-fuck her. He obliged, pumping his fingers in and out of where an unnerving hunger still burned red-hot. She continued blowing him, her mouth, hand, and tongue working frenziedly on him. A fine tremor seized his thighs when her tongue trailed down, licked his balls, and sucked them in to the moist heat of her mouth one at a time.

His fingers increased their pumping then, just as another orgasm encroached, eased out of her molten core and snuck, wet, toward her smaller opening, teasing the tight nerve-filled skin.

She froze. He'd never done that before. And she hadn't been brave enough to experiment before. His finger teased again.

Slightly weird sensation at first, but hell, it felt bloody good. He continued the caress, building her anticipation of the unexpected. Then he eased one finger inside the taut cavity . Sensation like she'd never known screamed through her. Lexi looked up at him, gasping, and found him watching her, his eyes blazing fiercely down at her.

"How does that feel?" he asked.

"Bloody fantastic," she muttered against his cock and planted another kiss on his rigid length. "Are you going to fuck me there?" The brave half of her hoped he would, the other half not so sure.

A cocky smile passed his lips. "Would you like me to?"

"Maybe, I don't know."

"Why don't you get used to my finger first, hmm? And then, if you're a good girl, we'll try something a bit more adventurous, deal?" he whispered. His finger probed again.

Slowly, she nodded. "Okay."

"Now, get back to work," he instructed, his cock nudging insistently against her cheek.

Eagerly she resumed her task, almost jerking off the bed when he slipped a second finger inside her pussy, double-holing her. Jesus, but it felt good.

"Fuck, the way you push your sweet ass against me... God, I'm dying to fuck you again."

"What are you waiting for?"

He paused, a concerned look on his face. "Are you sure?"

She nodded eagerly, unable to speak as his fingers drove her intuitively to the edge, waited until she was about to explode, and then withdrew and eased himself from her mouth. With a swift kiss, he pushed her back onto the bed.

Grabbing another condom, he slipped it on. "My turn on top, I think." He positioned his cock just inside of her, but held himself back, his eyes darkened until they were almost black with hunger and raw need.

"Now, Enzo," she moaned, clamped her legs around him and tried to force him deeper. He secured her arms above her head with one hand and cupped one plump breast in the other. Then he froze.

Anxious, she looked up and found his gaze focused on her scar. She tried to free her arm, but he held fast, his eyes raking the jagged line.

The next moment, he lowered his head, veiling his eyes as he licked around a tight aureola before sucking it into his hot mouth. He rocked his hips, teasing her, and all thought fled from her mind. Her thighs trembled with the power she exerted to force him inside her.

Finally, after gorging himself on her breasts, he thrust deep and buried himself to the hilt inside her.

Her greedy pussy welcomed him, eager muscles fastening around him to hold him to her.

"I love the way you squeeze me so tight," he breathed against her breast, his eyes fixed on hers once more, nothing but hot fierce desire reflected in their depths. "Those exquisite muscle contractions are a pure work of art."

She squeezed him tighter, expert inner muscles dancing along his length, eliciting a deep grunt and a helpless shudder from him.

"Christ, you can make me come just by doing that."

Lexi saw his pupils dilate with pleasure, and her own escalated. Unfortunately, it flooded her with liquid heat and caused her to lose a little grip on him. He took advantage, slid out, and rammed deep again. Her eyes fluttered shut as delirium took over.

"That's it, baby, lose it for me. Arch your back, scream for me," Enzo continued his hoarse litany, as, locked into his own rhythm, he slammed in and out of her.

Amid all the sensation storming through her, sadness well too.

Enzo never called her by her name; now, it was always *Baby* or, at times, Sweetheart. He hadn't called her Lexi for over a year, since back in London. She knew it was his way of creating emotional distance between them. That was fine by her. After all, look where all that emotional crap had gotten her. Chucked aside like yesterday's newspaper.

Baby was fine by her. If *Baby* got her *this*, she could live with it, she vowed, as another orgasm careened through her like a tidal wave before sucking her under.

Above her, Enzo continued to pump inside her. With his first, heady orgasm out of the way, he had time to pleasure her. Once he'd slowed his thrusts to accommodate her heady release, he let go of her arms, flipped her over onto her knees, and started all over again.

On and on it went, fuck after splendid fuck, orgasm after screaming orgasm, slamming into her again and again. He teased and held back, making her beg for him, but even he didn't escape the carnage. Every half hour or so, he shuddered through his own release. He'd bury his hands in her hair, sealing her lips with his as spasms shook his body.

For hours, they feasted on each other, until, in the early hours of the morning, she finally collapsed in a heap of nerveless exhaustion with Enzo's hard body caught in spasms beneath hers.

His sexual prowess always left her gobsmacked. And after six months of doing *this*, their passion showed no signs of abating. What they did in this room every Friday night had become a pivotal part of her existence. She craved it the way she craved air or sustenance. Without it, she feared she wouldn't be able to function. She would go through the rest of the week in a daze, a fog of contrived smiles and automatic responses honed from sheer survival-instinct.

But here her defenses were stripped bare.

Because in feeling alive again, she was reminded of the loss of the hopes and dreams she'd harbored. The fairytale existence that had been wiped out within a blink of an eye.

Lexi forced her mind from that painful memory. She had her work to occupy her now...

Work…

Vegas. Airport at ten.

Those were the last disjointed thoughts to pass through Lexi's mind before sleep claimed her.

Chapter Four

Enzo leaned on his elbow and looked down at the sleeping woman who'd broken his heart into a million tiny pieces.

How could she look so angelic, so sweetly sexy, and yet be so callous and unfeeling? In one single stroke, she'd shattered not only his life, but those of his sister's and two other women. He should hate her.

He *did* hate her.

Except, somehow, he couldn't live without her. Or rather, her brand of sex, which had him so hooked, half the time he didn't know whether he was going or coming. His lips twitched on a cynical smile. *Coming*, most likely, if the last four hours were anything to go by.

The first time they'd slept together, she'd been restrained, almost shy, until he'd coaxed her out of her shell. And boy, had she eventually exploded out of it.

Their second time together, *she'd been the one* ripping his clothes off, clawing his body with frenzied need, and vocalizing her every want. At first, he'd wondered whether the same woman shared his bed, until after her climax, she'd all but apologized for her behavior. He'd set her straight, telling her outright that he preferred her sassy, vampy side to the shy, virginal side she probably thought some men wanted. The pleasure of seeing her out of her shell made him, and his very eager cock, very happy indeed.

As it'd turned out, the rampant, screaming vixen hadn't been the only side she'd hidden from him.

She'd conveniently forgotten to mention she was a slut; not just a shameless slut, but a heartless one who hadn't seen anything wrong with fucking her ex on the side - the same ex, who also happened to be his sister's fiancé, Ian Pulbrook.

Enzo had found out after the accident after he'd decided to postpone their wedding. At the time, his instincts had warned that he was making a mistake; that he should be pulling the woman he loved closer, not pushing her away, no matter how irrational his sister was about any contact with Lexi.

True, Lexi had driven a little too fast that night. And true, the accident had left his sister physically and probably emotionally scarred for life. But as much as it'd hurt him to think Lexi had carelessly endangered his sister's life, he'd been sure that after a suitable period of healing, they could all move on with their lives, together.

Until the truth about her drinking came to light. He still remembered his horror when he'd found out that, although the other driver had been driving under the influence, Lexi herself had had a drink on the night of the accident.

Why had Lexi gotten behind the wheel knowing she'd been drinking? Why would she risk her life and those of his sister and friends in such a heartless way?

He'd asked her, when he'd finally been able to drag himself away from his sister the day after the accident. He'd hoped for some rational explanation for Lexi's behavior. At first, she'd tried to deny it, told him she'd only had a sip of the cocktail. But when he'd persisted, she'd confessed it had been more than a small sip. Truth be told, his trust in her had crumbled at that first lie.

Sure, she'd passed both the roadside Breathalyser test and the second test at the hospital, but that didn't keep him from believing that she was responsible for what had happened. It was no consolation that the other driver had been charged with "causing death by dangerous driving." Enzo couldn't help but believe that by having that drink, Lexi had reduced the reflexes needed to act quicker behind the wheel.

That reason made it hard to forgive her but he'd tried damned hard to because despite the horrific events and her part in it, he hadn't stopped loving her.

No, that particular gross error of judgment had bit him in the ass later. It'd bided its time, ready to destroy him, when a mere two days after the accident, he'd seen his beloved fiancé fucking Pulbrook, her ex; the same preppy asshole who'd dumped his sister along with her fairytale wedding plans.

Hate and deep bitterness had swamped him then.

He'd left London as soon as the doctors cleared Cara because he'd known if he stayed, he'd have ended up in jail for double homicide.

He'd brought Cara home, taken care of her by day, and fucked every woman in sight by night for two weeks straight until his best friend and business partner, Larry Morton, had knocked some sense into him.

When Larry had dragged him out of yet another hotel room, bleary-eyed, with yet another nameless bleached blonde with a face and body as dissimilar to Lexi's as he could find passed out on the bed, he'd realized he needed to get his act together.

He'd succeeded, or he thought he had, until Cara received a call from Fiona's parents with the news that Lexi had moved to LA and was asking permission to visit their daughter in the hospital.

It'd taken three days to calm Cara down. Her hysterical questioning of Lexi's motives resounded in his own head with an urgent need for an answer.

What the hell was she playing at, forcing them all to relive the horrific time?

With revived anger, he'd vowed to make her pay for what she'd done to Cara by whatever means necessary.

Only he hadn't needed to. He'd taken one look at her the first time he'd seen her at the hospital, seen the private hell of survivor's guilt she inhabited, and decided to leave her to it. Except along with the pain, he'd seen something else… A dark longing that lurked in the back of her eyes and thought, hell, maybe he could have a little revenge after all.

Obviously, Pulbrook hadn't done it for her, not the way he could.

He'd smiled around the fire that burned in his groin and seen the answering heat in her eyes. She'd sent him a text message the very next day and asked him if he wanted to meet for a drink.

He'd replied, no, he didn't want to meet for a drink. He'd sent a crude, succinct reply – *throw in a fuck and I'll think about it.*

Her reply – *where and when?* - had been immediate and surprised the hell out of him.

They'd met here ever since, in the penthouse he'd bought for them to live in after they were married but had never had the heart to sell, emotionlessly fucking their brains out every

Friday night. The hell remained visible in her eyes; the only time it disappeared was when she was caught in the throes of ecstasy.

He looked down, surprised his fingers had wound themselves into her hair.

Shit! He was getting his revenge--every time he made her scream out her orgasm, she paid him back a little for her betrayal. He should be happy.

He *was* happy. And when the time came to call a halt to this thing, he'd cut her off without a single thought. Original tit-for-fucking-tat.

She stirred beneath his hand as it roved over her silky-smooth rump, and he wondered whether to fuck her one last time before she left. His eager cock agreed with an impatient nudge. Hell, yeah.

Reaching for a condom in the almost-diminished pack, he slipped it on and slid on top of her. Enzo was between her thighs and inside her warm cunt before she came fully awake.

With a heartfelt sigh, she spread her legs wider for him. Another sigh, a soft dreamy cry of, "Oh, Enzo," and she was there with him, eager for another mind-blowing ride.

He must have fallen asleep afterward. Movement around the room pricked his consciousness, and he woke up to find her stepping into her clothes.

He jerked upright. Had she intended to leave without waking him? The residual anger he'd carried around since he found out about her Vegas trip surged again.

"What the hell are you doing?"

She looked up in surprise, then shrugged. "I think it's obvious, Enzo. I'm getting dressed."

"Why?"

"Because it's 3:30 a.m., and I have a flight to catch in a few hours."

He bit back the harsh words which rose to his lips and swung out of bed. If she wanted to leave, fine. He'd had more than his fill of her for the next seven days.

"What time do you leave for Vegas?" he asked, pulling on his boxers.

She shrugged on her jacket. "My flight's at eleven. I have to be at the airport at ten." She looked around for her hair clip, gave up, and ran her fingers through her hair.

The look of exhaustion on her face tugged at something inside that he didn't want to identify.

From nowhere, *take care of yourself*, sprang to his lips, but he forced them down. Why should he care what happened to her in Vegas? What he should be saying was, *Make sure you don't fuck anyone else while you're in Vegas or this thing between us is over.*

He didn't say that either. Exclusivity wasn't part of their deal. Changing the terms of the arrangement now would be unthinkable and smack of weakness on his part.

But would she? He eyed her, his gaze drawn to the delicate perfection of her face. Would she check into one of those hotels with the sleekly oiled cabana boys and indulge in a quick fuck behind the potted palms? Or would she pick up a guest for a night of mindless screwing?

Jesus, what the hell was he doing? Jealousy wasn't part of their deal either.

He pulled on his jeans and yanked up the zipper with more force than necessary. The images his mind threw up caused his jaw to clench in anger.

So, he didn't trust her. Damned straight. Look where trust had gotten him last time.

But it pissed him off at how deeply she'd embedded herself under his skin, so rampantly in his blood that he would count the minutes, hell, the seconds until Friday night rolled around again.

"You ready?" he snapped, although he saw for himself she was. Her head jerked in his direction and wariness crept into her eyes.

"Yes. I am."

He pulled her to him, rammed a savage kiss on her lips and stepped away. "Let's go." Grasping her elbow, he steered her out the door and smashed down the part of him that screamed to hold on and never let her go.

He knew better.

Once bitten, hell, never again.

Chapter Five

The plane landed at McCarran International just after midday on Friday morning. Lexi bit her lip at her body's tenderness as she reached up for her carry-on. Thankfully, there weren't many people in business class to witness her gingerly stride out of the plane.

She still couldn't believe how animalistic, almost primitive, Enzo had been in bed last night.

He'd always been a powerful, earthy lover, but sex with him had never been the ruthless, feral coupling of last night. She'd barely had a moment to breathe before he'd been ready again, demanding, and receiving, a consuming performance from her. She hadn't asked what had bugged him last night-- talk simply wasn't on their agenda when they met up.

No, their time together was all about sex, where the only words spoken were meant to enhance the sex; make it hotter, steamier. Enzo loved it when she vocalized her demands in bed, and he in turn vocalized his. Apart from maybe a *hello* and *goodbye* as a nod to civility, they barely spoke outside of the bedroom.

Except last night, when Enzo had introduced another dimension to their sexcapade - sex with more than a hint of dominance and a whole lot of anger.

In the clear light of day, Lexi berated herself for not standing up to him.

Whatever had gotten him into that state had nothing to do with her. She shouldn't have tolerated it. But God, the experience had been phenomenal!

She inhaled sharply. Nevertheless, she concluded as she wheeled her carry-on toward the exit, it had been wrong to give in to him. Wrong to let him march her down the hall into the elevator afterward, his fury palpable, tingeing the air around them. Wrong for him to kiss her again, hard and deep against her car, before shoving her inside and striding away with taut instruction to drive safely thrown over his shoulder.

First thing next Friday, when they met up again, she'd set him straight. Never again would she allow control to be wrested from her, the way it had a year ago. She'd agreed to their tryst because she knew what it entailed - punishment on his part for what she'd done to his sister and an inexplicable need to stay connected with the man she still craved on hers. She wasn't sure what name to hang on it, but she didn't think it was love. Hell, why would she love a man who would dump her without so much as a word?

He'd paid her a visit the day after the accident; he'd kept his anger at bay as he demanded to know why she'd drank that night. Sure, at first she'd tried to bullshit her way out of it, but in the end she'd come clean. The disappointment in his eyes had scared her a little, but never in her wildest dreams had she thought it would spell the end of their relationship.

She'd taken his request to push back their wedding simply as a chance to give Cara time to recover from the accident. And why would he tell her he'd see her the next day, even kiss her, when he knew he was leaving London?

Her own desperate heartache still had the power to deliver gut-wrenching pain when she recalled just *how* she'd found out her engagement had ended.

After days locked in a fog of pain, the realization that Enzo hadn't come back to see her had finally penetrated her stunned senses. Endless calls with no reply had driven her to seek him out at his house.

The realtor's pitying look and insouciant tones as she informed her that Enzo's rented house was back on the market because he'd returned to the States still made her skin tighten with humiliation. She'd crawled back into bed and stayed there for a solid week, until her grandmother's anxious entreaties had forced her to pull herself together.

But that was then. She was much stronger now.

Any more caveman tactics from Enzo and she walked. Plain and simple.

Fendi sunglasses firmly in place, she walked into the bright Vegas sunlight, ignoring the avid gazes that her voluptuous figure gloved in a mint green skirt suit attracted. She tried to shift her mind into work mode as the car service town car drew up beside her.

Nine viewings in the next two days was definitely pushing it. After which, she'd need to make a shortlist of four or five properties and present the portfolio to her clients. Then on Monday, she'd take them around, arrange second viewings where necessary on Tuesday, and then leave them to decide which property they wanted.

As an international relocation consultant, Lexi had found homes for hundreds of clients all over the world. She'd started as a small-time relocator with a firm in South London, and then moved to Kingfisher Realtors, after being recognized for her innate ability to fit the right people to the right homes.

She knew she had a natural talent, but it wasn't until her short stint on a TV property show that she'd gained international acclaim. Overnight, she'd become the go-to person, topping the list as *the* property hunter for celebrities and *Fortune 500* clients.

Initially, the success had gone to her head, until she realized she'd be dealing with monumental egos and self-important minions who thought she should be paying *them* for the privilege of her services.

More and more, she missed the fulfillment of finding the right house for young couples and first-time buyers, seeing the sheer joy on their faces as they secured the humble homes they'd most likely live in, bring up their children in, and grow old in.

Instead, she had to contend with locating and negotiating the best price for the next "in" place for egotistical CEOs, aging rockers and their starlet wives, or even worse, their drug-stoked offspring who wanted to live in the same neighborhood as Kim K or Britney. Of course, the minute Kim moved, Lexi had to be on the next flight, hunting down a penthouse, chalet, or villa.

Before the accident last year, when she'd looked forward to living her own happily-ever-after as Mrs. Enzo Saldana, Lexi had toyed with the idea of going back to her roots, starting her own company in LA, and catering to couples and families looking for their first homes. Then all her dreams had crashed and burned. At first, she'd thought she could remain in London after Enzo left, but even that option had been cruelly torn from her.

Ian Pulbrook had seen to that.

Kingfisher's offer of a position in LA had been a godsend and she'd taken it, allowing her gratefully numbed senses to retreat further from the horror that had become her life.

She wrenched her thoughts from the dark vacuum of remembrance and pushed her shades up her nose when the Strip came into view. The spectacular sights and themed hotels flashed past and, even in daylight, the world-famous Las Vegas strip was a sight to behold. She'd only visited twice before, the first time when *Ocean's Eleven* had propelled every A- and B-listed star to acquire a suite at the *Bellagio*.

The second had been when the *Wynn Hotel* had opened; its sheer opulence and decadence had prompted another frenzied bid for space within its hallowed walls.

This time, she was in search of a condo for a non-celebrity couple, a *Mr. and Mrs. Johnson*, the brief said. Although she had her suspicions that there might be another, more legitimate Mrs. Johnson tucked away in the background. For one thing, *Mr. Johnson*, a filthy rich wine merchant originally from Napa, was old enough to be the grandfather of the *Mrs. Johnson* she'd met, and everything about her screamed high-class hooker. Lexi had a feeling she was hunting for a dirty weekend get-away pad, not the alleged retirement home for the couple.

But hers wasn't to reason why, she mused cynically, as the car pulled up in front of her hotel.

First a light lunch, followed by a read through of her papers and phone calls to the local realtors confirming her appointments. Then a massage and a relaxed evening to ready herself for the hectic pace of the next few days.

Saturdays were busy days for realtors, especially in a fast-moving market like Vegas. In a city where fortunes were made and lost in the blink of an eye, one always had to be ready to move quickly. The condo or suite, which you'd been warned would never be sold, could suddenly come on the market and be gone within a matter of hours.

She thanked her driver and followed the bellhop to the front desk.

"Hello, Ms. Mayfield. Good to have you with us again. We gave you your usual suite, here's your keycard, and your massage has been booked for four as requested."

Lexi smiled inwardly at the very American efficiency. If there was one thing she loved about Americans, it was their skills in the hospitality business.

"Thank you. Would it be possible to move the massage to three, instead?" she asked, thinking of the aches she had in unmentionable places.

"Of course." The attractive blonde behind the desk replied smoothly. "We've also arranged for the same masseuse for you. I believe you used Hans the last time?"

"I don't remember his name." Oh, but she did. She recalled Hans and his amazing assets as clear as day. "I'm sure whoever you send will be fine."

Perfect teeth gleamed in her perfect face. "Thank you, Ms. Mayfield. Here's your wi-fi card. Enjoy your stay."

"Thank you." She took the card and followed the bellhop to the elevator.

Riding up to her floor, Lexi hid her smile as the spectacular image of Hans rose in her mind. She hadn't experienced his personal brand of massage in well over six months. If he'd lasted this long on the job, then he must be very discreet indeed.

Handing over a twenty-dollar tip to the bellhop, she shut the door behind him and surveyed her room. A junior suite with clear views of the Strip, it was decorated in honeyed tones of cream and gold, with a whirlpool bath and separate shower adjoining the bedroom on one side. On the other, a small sitting room held the music and drinks console and a desk where she could plug in her laptop. This she did, removing her clothes as it booted up.

Crossing the room to the phone, she ordered a club sandwich and fries, forgoing the salad she'd originally contemplated. She was starving, especially after that sexathon last night and only a coffee and half a bagel for breakfast this morning.

Her gaze moved to her bag. Should she call and tell Enzo she'd arrived safely?

Hell, no. He'd think she was keeping tabs on him or something. The last thing she wanted was to appear needy.

It was about the sex for them. Nothing else.

Remember that, Lexi.

After a quick shower, she slipped on the hotel robe. Aside from her bra and panties there was no need to dress; she'd only have to undress again for her massage. Her breasts tingled against the soft cotton and she experienced a sense of disquiet at her body's behavior. When had she become so sex mad? For fuck's sake, her body still throbbed from last night's exploits, yet here she was, barely able to breathe as she recalled Enzo's hands on her body.

Already she could feel the slick moisture between her swelling labia, and even the brush of loosened hair across her nape caused desire to shoot to her groin.

Focus Lexi, she berated herself. Grabbing her case, she spread the papers on the bed, sorting them by address and grouping them by area. Halfway through assessing each viewing, her lunch arrived. By the time she'd placed the calls to the respective realtors and inputted the details into her smart phone, she'd polished off her meal. She'd have to work that off later in the hotel gym, but for now she padded to her small balcony, coffee in hand, and looked out over the Strip.

The knock on the door came a few minutes later.

Turning, she took a deep breath and went to open it.

"Miss Mayfield, it's good to see you again."

"Hello, Hans. Come on in," she invited, striving to sound cool and collected, even though her senses tweaked at the sight of the man in front of her. Although dressed in the loose short white tunic and matching trousers used by the staff at the health spa, the uniform didn't detract from the amazing physique beneath. His packed muscles moved fluidly as he wheeled his folded massage table inside the room. As he went back to the door to fetch his bag, Lexi's eyes dropped to his tight ass. She swallowed at the bunching muscles. God, he was hot! Almost as hot as—

"Would you like to take the robe off?"

He'd returned and proceeded to set up the massage bed. When he finished, he stood back with a towel over his arm, gazing at her. "Lie face down for me, please." His Scandinavian accent was still pronounced, and the way he spoke carefully somehow made her want to smile. She gave in and smiled; God knows, she had nothing to smile about these days.

But the recollection of Hans's not so precise pronunciation the last time she'd been with him resurrected the imp inside her.

Keeping her eyes on his, she dropped the robe and walked in her bra and panties toward the massage bed. With slow movements, she climbed up and did as he instructed, her gaze on his face as he took in her body. Beneath his trousers, she saw his cock thicken and her smile widened.

Darling Hans. How she'd missed him. He'd been so good to her the last time. For a short while, he'd banished her nightmares and made her feel that the world wasn't such a cold, dark place.

Turning to face the towel he held up, she undressed completely, then she watched him ready the oils. He chose and poured a healthy amount of eucalyptus oil into his palm and move toward her. Their gazes locked as he stood next to the bed, his hands poised.

"Is there anywhere you'd like me to concentrate on, Miss Mayfield?"

"I'm tense all over," she replied softly, her gaze dropping to his erection. "A bit like you," she finished cheekily.

When she looked at him, his grey eyes were ablaze with desire. Without a word, he inclined his head.

"If you would rest your hands on either side of you, I shall get to work."

Again his precise tone, coupled with his mounting erection, brought a smile to her face in recollection of the previous time. How many women had he done that with? Countless, most likely.

His firm hands set to work, kneading the knots out of her tense flesh. Sighing, she closed her eyes, totally relaxed as his expert hands eased her stress. She was almost drifting into sleep when she sensed his presence at her shoulder.

"I've missed you," he breathed in her ear, his hands sliding between her shoulder blades and up her neck.

She smiled, but kept her eyes closed. "I've missed you too, Hans."

His hands slid smoothly into her hair, performing the stress-relieving Indian head massage he knew she loved. A helpless moan escaped her and she gave herself up to it.

Several minutes later, he moved back down to her shoulders, soothing his hands down her spine, before instructing, "Turn over for me, please."

She opened her eyes and found him looking down at her, the desire unabated in his eyes. Slowly she turned, conscious of his gaze on her body. Her nipples puckered and his attention zeroed in on her reaction. He swallowed, his cock nudging against the soft material of his trousers. Silently, he stepped forward and began his ministrations. By now she felt boneless, although a lazy curl of heat continued winding its way through her. Then he slid his palms between her breasts and brought his face close to hers.

"Would you like total relaxation, Miss Mayfield?" he whispered, his gaze on her lips.

Lexi looked back at him. Would she? The last time he'd asked her that, she'd been in turmoil, seeking oblivion. Her answer had been yes, and he'd shown her an amazing two hours. But now? Her body was ready; she could feel the slickness between her legs; she could let him fuck her, as he was dying to. After all, she didn't have an exclusivity clause with Enzo. He didn't own her body or her mind. She could fuck whomever she chose.

Her gaze dropped to his erection, recalling its velvety thickness.

She inhaled deeply and stepped away from temptation.

It was wrong. She didn't have Enzo, or any exclusivity rights to speak of, but she didn't need Hans as she had the last time. Having sex with him now would just be taking advantage of a situation she was trying to move past. She also got the feeling her masseuse carried a soft spot for her, one which with the slightest encouragement could grow into something else. She wasn't ready for that. Would probably never be.

Raising a gentle hand to his cheek, she looked into his kind eyes and smiled. "You were wonderful to me the last time, just when I needed a kind soul, and I'll never forget it. That's the main reason I asked for you today; to say thank you. You're a kind and generous man." She dropped her hand. "But not this time. I'm sorry."

Disappointment flashed through his eyes, but he stayed where he was. "There is someone else," he stated, a rueful smile curving his lips.

Was Enzo her *someone else*? Not even close. But to keep things simple, she nodded.

"Is he good for you?"

Her smile slipped. "No. He's very, very bad for me."

His gaze turned contemplative. "But he's what you need?"

God! Such simple words, but their accuracy summed up her life. She needed Enzo to keep her from the abyss that threatened to suck her down. "Yes, he's what I need."

Hans nodded, slowly straightened, and resumed the massage. When he finished, he laid a warm towel over her.

"Did you know that the lack of hair in the pubic area is said to enhance sexual pleasure?"

Smiling again, she closed her eyes. "I've heard, but I don't believe it."

"I know this for a fact. I have noticed the difference with my girlfriend. If you like, I can wax you?"

Her eyes popped open. Hans stared back at her, his face deadly serious. The urge to break into hysterical giggles seized her, whether from Hans standing there talking about his girlfriend while sporting a hard-on for her, or the fact that he wanted to shave her pubes off, she wasn't sure. The closest she'd ever come was a bikini wax. She'd never bothered with anything more extreme since Enzo had mentioned he loved her curls.

Now she thought about it and smiled. Why not? Didn't philosophers say to try everything once?

"All right then. Go for it."

Half an hour later, he stood back and smiled at his handiwork. "Beautiful. You look beautiful down there."

Musing at the surrealistic nature of the whole thing, she took the mirror he held out and examined herself. The sight of her clit and labia peeking between her legs was so unexpected, she gasped. Heat flooded her. The thought of

Enzo seeing her like this turned her on even more. She handed the mirror back, suddenly eager to be rid of him.

"Thank you very much, Hans. You've been great." She made a mental note to leave him a huge tip when she checked out.

Half-impatient, she watched him gather his equipment. Finally, she followed him to the door. He paused and turned back to her. "I can come back tonight and give you a Tantric massage, if you like. It can be very fulfilling and relaxing also."

She shook her head. "Thanks, but no. This one's done the trick. I haven't smiled in a long time, but you made me smile today. It was very good to see you."

"You too, Miss Mayfield. I am moving to LA in a few weeks. Maybe I can get in touch, give you some more massages?"

"Yeah, that would be great." Stifling a sigh, she plucked a business card from her bag and handed it to him. "Call me when you're in town."

She closed the door and rushed to the bathroom. Shedding her robe, she stood in front of the mirror. Why did the sight of her shaven mound turn her on so much? Tentative fingers strayed down, touched, and she gasped at the sensitivity of her skin. Would Enzo like it?

Her blood thrummed. If Hans was right, she'd just been handed a whole new avenue of pleasure. Suddenly, she couldn't wait to get back to LA.

The thought scared her a little.

***

Lexi entered her apartment, dropped her travel case on the floor beside the door, and lobbed the keys onto the table.

The trip had been a resounding success. The Johnsons had taken one look at the third property she'd shown them and immediately fallen in love with it. Caution against using their heads instead of their hearts when buying property had finally, grudgingly, led them to agree to a second viewing the next day. Luckily, they'd felt the same; or rather *Mrs. Johnson* had managed to convince old Mr. Johnson it was the right property for them. They'd put a down payment on it there and then, and left Lexi to finalize the purchase.

She'd gotten the transaction underway this morning before boarding the plane and, with any luck, the Johnsons would take possession of their brand new condo in four weeks' time.

In the kitchen, she extracted a bottle of water from the fridge and poured herself a glass. First water, then a much needed shower. Her flight had been delayed for an hour, and the jeans and midriff-baring top she'd worn for comfort now felt sticky and unbearable. Weary, she set down the glass and headed into the living room. The flashing light on her answering machine made her pause. She rarely received calls on her landline unless... Cautioning herself not to think the worst, she crossed over and pressed the button.

The tremulous voice on the machine sent shivers of apprehension down her spine.

"Lexi, it's Mrs. Harding, Fiona's mom. I'm at the hospital. Th-there's been a change. When you get this message please call me on—"

With shaking hands, she replayed the message, grabbed the phone, and punched in the number. The cell phone rang once and went to voice mail. Cursing, she tried again, her insides twisting in savage knots. When it went to voice mail a second time, she hung up and reached for her cell phone where she kept the hospital number on speed dial. Her trembling fingers impeded her so much, she had to try three times. When the hospital operator came on line, her voice came out in a croaky rasp.

"Neurological wing, please," she said in a rush, and then tried to take deep breaths as the call was redirected.

A harried voice came on the line. "Nurses' station."

"This is Lexi Mayfield. Can you tell me the condition of Miss Fiona Harding, please?" she shot out without preamble.

Silence greeted her request and all she heard for interminable seconds was a rustle of paper on the other end. Gritting her teeth, she fought the urge to scream.

Finally, the nurse spoke. "I don't have a Lexi Mayfield listed as family, so I can't give out confidential details of the patient."

"No, you don't understand. I'm—" What? A friend of a friend, whose sole presence in Fiona's life had been a short-lived acquaintanceship that had ended in total disaster? In desperation, she asked, "Is Nurse Simpson working today?" The older woman knew her, so maybe Lexi could convince her to bend the rules, just this once.

The nurse gave an impatient sigh, clearly of the opinion that Lexi was a time waster. "No, she doesn't start her shift until four."

Lexi glanced at her watch unnecessarily, very much aware that it was the middle of the afternoon. She grabbed her bag. The only way to get answers would be to get to the hospital as soon as she could.

"Can you tell me if Ms. Harding's parents are still there?"

"Like I said I—"

"Can't give out any information. Fine. Thank you." *For nothing.*

She slammed the phone down and rushed to the door, her thoughts in turmoil. In the hallway, she tried Mrs. Harding's number again, but got the same voice mail message. This time, Lexi left a message to say she was on her way. With no cell phones allowed in the hospital, she doubted Fiona's mother would get the message, nevertheless...

Forty minutes later, she arrived at St Jude's. The mid-afternoon traffic for once had been blessedly light. Lexi hurried into the building and stabbed an impatient finger for the elevator. Once it creaked its way down and opened, she rushed in and stabbed the button again for the seventh floor. As it rose, so did her heart, until it lodged in her throat. Her eyes burned with the need to cry, but she blinked rapidly. Tears were no use. What she needed to do now was pray.

Like floodgates released, a torrent of prayers flooded her mind, speeding through like a bullet train. *Please, please God, let her be all right. I can't take another tragedy. I'll do anything...Please don't let her die because of me. Please, please...*

She opened her eyes as the elevator doors opened and stepped out into an empty corridor. *The corridors are never empty.* For some reason this made her heart pound harder. Tightening her hands on her handbag straps, she walked on shaky legs to the nurse's station, which stood unmanned.

Please, please God…

She bit her lip to stop a whimper of despair. Gaze riveted on the last door, she walked toward it, her breath loud and harsh in the quiet space.

As she approached, she heard muted voices, whispering from within.

Taking a deep breath, she knocked softly and entered.

Margaret and Gary Harding sat next to their daughter's bed, their eyes on her face.

Lexi's own gaze zeroed in on Fiona. She lay as Lexi had left her on Thursday – still and unmoving. Desperate, she checked for signs of life. Icy hands curled around her heart. The ventilator was off and her intubator had been removed.

No!

Whatever sound she made caused the older couple to look her way. Steeling herself against their pain, she forced herself to look at them, while inside, her heart tore with agony.

"I—I'm so, so sorry. I know it'll never be enough, but please I want you to know how sorry…" She choked and her throat closed up. Tears filled her eyes. The hand she lifted to swipe at them felt cold and numb.

God, what had she done? Another life ended because of her!

Her heart clenched further when she saw different emotions cross their faces – anxiety, sadness. Pain.

Mrs. Harding motioned her forward. Lexi tried to shake her head, but Fiona's mother beckoned harder.

She went forward and allowed her hand to be taken by Margaret's.

Swallowing around the lump in her throat, she tried to continue, "I'm so sorry, Mrs. Harding. I…I went out of town…just got back and heard your message. I—I tried to call, but they wouldn't give me any information."

"I know, I should have said more, but I've never liked answering machines, and I don't have your cell number so…"

Lexi tightened her grip on the older woman's hand. "I'm so sorry. I'll never forgive myself, never." She heard the wobble in her voice as she fought back the tears. *Please, please...help me be strong for them...please.*

The other woman's eyes filled with tears, and Lexi felt her heart break. Why was this happening? Her eyes went to Fiona's still, pale face, struggling to find the words to express the emotion locked inside. From a distance, she heard Maggie speak and tried to focus.

"Oh, please don't cry, Lexi. It's good news, or at least we hope to have good news by tomorrow. You see, Fiona woke up this morning."

Chapter Six

Lexi closed the door to Fiona's room with unsteady hands, and finally allowed the tears she'd held back to fall. Now thankful for the empty corridor, she slid down onto the floor, buried her face in her hands and gave in to her quiet sobs.

Her prayers had been answered!

"Fiona's not out of the woods yet, but the doctors are optimistic with the results of her initial tests. Another batch of tests had been ordered and they'll know more in the morning." Those had been Margaret's words.

According to her, Fiona had just opened her eyes while the nurse had been checking her vital signs this morning.

"That's just like Fiona, to frighten the living daylights out of that poor nurse! Anyway, the nurse asked her to blink if she knew who she was and understood what the nurse was saying, and she did," Fiona's mom had related through her tears. "Half an hour later, she went back into her coma, but the doctors assure us it sometimes happens. The brain scan shows heightened activity and they're optimistic she'll come round fully in the next twenty-four to forty-eight hours."

Lexi fished a tissue out of her bag and blew her nose. She'd wanted to stay longer but recognized their desire to be alone with their daughter. Maggie had assured her she'd let Lexi know if anything happened, and she'd gratefully grasped the promise.

Physically and emotionally drained, she pulled herself away from the wall and made her way to the nurse's station. Nurse Simpson looked up from her charts and smiled.

"Ah, there you are child. I just got in and heard the good news. I hope those are tears of joy?"

Lexi's smile wobbled. "Yes, they certainly are."

"Well, all right then. Now, get yourself home, you look exhausted. There's nothing you can do now but wait."

Lexi nodded, fresh tears stinging her eyes. She approached the desk and, after a moment's hesitation, handed over her business card. "Nurse Simpson, I know I'm not family, but would you be kind enough to call me if anything changes before morning?"

The nurse tucked the card into her pocket. "Don't worry, sweet pea, I will. And in my opinion, your selfless devotion makes you part of the family. Now, don't start crying again. We'll take good care of your friend. Just get yourself home and look after yourself now."

"Thank you, Nurse Simpson."

"Call me Ada," she invited with another smile.

"Thanks, Ada. See you later."

With much lighter steps than she'd arrived with, Lexi walked to the elevator and pressed the button. The slow response made her debate whether to take the stairs. Surely in a hospital as advanced as this, someone in administration could authorize an overhaul of such an outdated elevator? She breathed a sigh of relief when it finally arrived.

Only when the doors opened, she wished with all her heart she *had* taken the stairs.

Enzo, Cara, and a doctor occupied the small space. Cara was the first to see her. Enzo, facing away from her, was deep in conversation with the doctor.

At her outraged gasp, the other two men looked up. Enzo's gaze locked with hers and everything fell away. A myriad of sensations tumbled one after the other through her.

The shock, surprise, and intense lust she glimpsed in his eyes echoed her own feelings, but the anger she couldn't reciprocate. Like a hypnosis patient following the swing of a stopwatch, she followed his gaze when it darted to his sister and returned to her. Cold indifference replaced the anger, and her heart plummeted further.

The doors started to slide shut. She did nothing to stop it, her gaze still riveted on Enzo.

From the corner of her eye, she saw the doctor leap forward to stay the doors. "Uh, you coming in? If you're going down, I suggest you grab this one or it'll be at least a week before the next one comes along."

She tore her gaze from Enzo's. Her heart went out to the doctor who was clearly uncomfortable with the palpable tension in the air.

Barely able to speak around the lump in her throat, she shook her head. "It's okay. I—I'll take the stairs." She should've done that in the first place. God, her recent fit of crying must have left her looking like a puffed up scarecrow.

She fought a strong urge to run a quick hand through her hair and sucked in a breath at Enzo's hiss of impatience. Shifting her gaze to him, she saw his lips pressed together in a tight, formidable line. "Get in the elevator. You're going down, so are we. We're all adults here."

Insisting on taking the stairs would be childish on Lexi's part. Her eyes darted to Cara, but she'd turned away, her dark hair covering half her face.

On shaky legs, she stepped forward and entered the elevator, then turned her back on its three occupants. When the doors shut, locking them in, she held her breath and silently urged the ancient contraption to move quicker.

She jumped when Enzo's voice sounded right next to her ear.

"Which floor? First?"

The heat of his breath against her bare shoulder raised gooseflesh all over her body, reminding her of how he loved to blow on her clit before he tortured it with his tongue. When he leaned forward, one finger poised over the buttons, she forgot to breathe. Cold green eyes slid over her face, one eyebrow cocked in cool enquiry.

With a swallow, she nodded and stepped away slightly when he straightened. Expecting him to take his place back at his sister's side, her temperature rose further when he remained next to her. Behind her, she could feel Cara's hatred wash over her. Damn, she *really* should have taken the stairs.

Unable to take it anymore, she broke the silence. "It's good news about Fiona, isn't it?"

Enzo's lips tightened. A deep, "Yeah, it's great," rumbled from his chest. Cara remained silent.

The doctor, obviously seizing a chance to lighten the mood, stepped forward. "Ah, are you talking about Miss Harding? The news of her amazing recovery is all over the hospital. Are you also a friend of hers?"

"No, she's not," Cara snapped, her voice raw with loathing. "She's—"

"Cara." Enzo's sharp warning ramped the tension to breaking point. So much so that when the elevator jostled to a stop, Lexi first thought her nerves had snapped. Sensing freedom, she stepped forward to escape from the unbearable box only to realize they were on the third floor.

"Right, this is us, I think." The doctor's relief was blatant. "It was good to meet you, uh…?"

"Lexi. Mayfield," she supplied after clearing the lump in her throat.

"I'm Dr. Hopkirk." He gave her a puzzled smile as he stepped out.

Her smile slipped as Enzo speared her with another heat-filled look. Hot lust tightened the knots in her belly. He inclined his head, exited, and waited for his sister. Cara slipped past her, the side of her scarred faced averted as the three disappeared down the corridor.

The hand Lexi raised to stab the button trembled uncontrollably. The doors slid shut and, for the second time in a very short time, she sagged against the wall of the elevator.

Helpless tears rose in her eyes. With sickening clarity, she realized that no matter what good came of the tragedy, Enzo and Cara would never forgive her for the accident. It seemed not even Fiona's miraculous recovery was enough to soften the hearts of the two people who had once been the center of her world.

How could Enzo look at her as if she he couldn't stand the sight of her while at the same time fucking her with his eyes? Knowing he hated her for the almost fatal attraction they seemed to have for each other hurt deeply, but somehow in the privacy of their Friday night trysts, it had been…not okay, but almost tolerable.

In the glaring light of day, however, his barely veiled animosity was unbearable. A fat tear rolled down her cheek; she did nothing to stop it. She knew she wept for the lost love she'd secretly nurtured, the love which had once held so much promise, so much hope.

She could've made him so happy, she knew it in her bones. Her tongue thickened as more tears fell. A flood of shame swamped Lexi when she realized part of her had prayed for Fiona's recovery because she'd secretly hoped that it might heal the rift between Enzo and her. Now, that particular dream had shown itself to be just a figment of her imagination.

The elevator finally touched down. With each step toward her car, she knew the decision had to be made; she had to face the hard truth and walk away from Enzo once and for all.

***

Enzo stood at the third floor window to the private visitor's room and watched Lexi approach her car. Anger and savage lust raged through him in equal measures. How could she have callously ruined something so beautiful as the love they'd shared and still manage to look like the wounded party?

Seeing her outside the elevator just now with deep shadows under eyes, dried tracks of tears on her face, had nearly ripped him in two. Never before had he fought such a forceful instinct to take her in his arms and soothe away her pain. He forced himself to remember that she'd been the author of her own pain - of all their pain. By fucking someone else, giving away what he'd thought had been exclusively his, she'd broken something he'd thought was precious.

But a few minutes ago, she'd looked as if her whole world was about to cave in on her.

He also knew he was being delusional. Her weariness was most likely from her trip to Vegas. And if she'd cried over Fiona, then at least it showed there was some humanity in her after all. Any sympathy he had should be directed to his sister and the huge decision she faced right now.

Lexi didn't need him, nor did she deserve any support from him. Hell, even with her tiredness, she still managed to look a knockout. He'd barely managed to stop himself from ripping Dr. Hopkirk's eyes out when he'd seen him checking out Lexi's ass in the elevator.

It seemed any man who came within a mile of Lexi immediately got a hard on. And yeah, the thought more than pissed him off.

With clenched fists, he watched her sinuous body slide into her car and drive off, then immediately wished he was with her.

Shaking his head at the sheer lunacy of his thoughts, he whirled away from the window.

He really needed to have his head examined. His sister needed him now. With Fiona waking up, the past would be dredged up again, and Cara's sensitive emotions would have to be handled with kid gloves. His sister had been through enough pain to last her a lifetime.

But dammit, right now every foolish nerve in his body yearned to be back in the penthouse with Lexi, never mind that it was only Tuesday and not Friday.

He craved her with a hunger that was slowly driving him insane. Many times over the last couple of days he'd toyed with calling her just to hear her voice.

How fucking needy and pathetic was that?

Crossing to the coffee machine which dispensed burnt, tasteless coffee, he poured himself a cup. He stared into the dark liquid and finally admitted it - the woman was a drug in his blood, and the cure was rarer than he'd imagined. The past five days he'd thought of little else but her, even when his mind should've been on business.

Larry, his long-suffering partner, fed up with his lack of attention to his job, had read him the riot act after a disastrous business meeting this morning with a stern warning to *get a grip*. That he'd grasped the opportunity and immediately contemplated meeting Lexi's plane at the airport had angered him so much he'd driven in the opposite direction to his gym, intent on pounding the shit out of a punching bag until one of them broke.

He'd never made it. The call from Cara about Fiona had come as he'd walked through the door of his gym. He expected his sister to be a basket case when he arrived. But she'd been the opposite.

If anything, Cara had seemed to emerge, albeit in a small way, from the embittered state she'd inhabited for the last year. She'd even smiled for the first time today.

And then she'd dropped a bombshell at Enzo's feet.

Which was why he was here in a waiting room, drinking crappy coffee, supporting his baby sister as she took the first tentative steps toward a possible corrective facial surgery she'd decided to undergo.

The door opened. He looked up in relief as she entered, followed by Dr. Hopkirk.

"Everything all right?" he directed his question at the doctor.

"I've taken some skin samples and I'll run some tests overnight. We should know more tomorrow. But at this stage, I'm hopeful."

"You sure about doing this, sis? The decision was rather sudden, wasn't it?"

The look that passed between doctor and patient tweaked his radar.

Dr. Hopkirk cleared his throat. "Actually, it's not. I've been seeing your sister for a few weeks now."

Enzo started. "*Seeing her*?"

The young doctor flushed. "No, no, not that way. I meant, we met when I treated Miss Harding's leg burns. I saw your sister's injuries and…well, I've had a hard time convincing her to let me take a look." His eyes strayed to Cara and stayed. "She approached me today and agreed, finally."

Enzo followed his gaze. "Just like that? Cara, are you sure?"

She nodded, hesitant at first, but then a rare light of determination shone in her eyes. "If it's possible, I'm willing to give it a try."

Hopkirk smiled. "That's the spirit. I'll give you a call tomorrow when I have the results and we'll schedule you for another consult, all right?"

She nodded.

Enzo shook hands with the doctor and turned to her. "Come on, let's get you home."

In silence, they walked out into the corridor.

"I'm really proud of you, you know. Whatever help you need, I'll be there for you." He pulled her close into a hug.

"I'll hold you to that," she murmured before pulling away. "Let's take the stairs. That damn elevator takes too long."

Enzo fell into step beside her, but with the mention of the elevator, his mind flew miles away. Or not far enough away, depending on which way he looked at it. He shouldn't be wondering whether Lexi was home by now; shouldn't be wondering what she was doing. It was Tuesday, not Friday.

But maybe he could call her. They'd made an exception last week, maybe she'd be too hot for him to wait until Friday.

"…don't you think?"

He tuned and found Cara's quizzical gaze on him.

"Sorry, what did you say?"

"I said, Lexi had a lot of balls showing up here today, don't you think?"

He suppressed a sigh at the familiar belligerent tone. "I'm sure she came because she was contacted by Fiona's parents, much the same way you were."

"Yeah, but she could've said no. She could've waited until tomorrow. Anyone with an ounce of sensitivity wouldn't have turned up. Talk about rubbing it in everyone's face."

He frowned. "That's a bit harsh, don't you think?"

"But Fiona's parents are still here. The last thing they need to see the very day she wakes up is the person who put their daughter in a coma. I mean how insensitive is that?"

"Technically, the accident wasn't her fault, Cara. The truck came from the other side of the road and hit her car, remember? Besides, with things looking up for Fiona, maybe her parents are ready to put the tragedy behind them?" he suggested, hoping she'd drop the subject.

"Or maybe Lexi just doesn't know when to quit."

Frustration ate at him. Scrubbing a hand over his face, he stopped. "I don't understand you, Cara. You were upset last week when you thought she was leaving town. Now you're upset because she's still in LA. What exactly do you want?"

"I want to be able to turn back time. For me not to look like this!" She shoved her hand in her face. "For everything to go back to the way it was! Is that too much to ask?" she shouted as tears swam into her eyes.

Swallowing his anger, he enfolded her in his arms, her cry of pain ripping through him. "No, it's not, and I'm sorry for what happened to you. But we can't turn back time, Cara. All we can do is move forward. Look, the main thing is that she came because Fiona woke up. *Fiona* is who we should be concerned about. She's out of her coma and signs show she's going to be all right. Let's be thankful about that, okay?"

She sniffed, bunching her hand in his T-shirt. "Yes, but all I'm saying is, Lexi could've shown some tact. And did you see what she was wearing, showing off her body like that—"

He dropped his arms, knowing what was coming next. "Enough already. Seriously, I don't want to fight about Lexi again. All right?"

She shoved him away, aggression ramped high. "Who says I want to fight?"

"Well, somehow we always end up fighting when her name comes up."

"That's because you always defend her when I talk about her."

He suppressed another sigh. "No, I don't and you know it. You're my family. *You're* the most important person in my life. And because I know she upsets you, I don't want you to get riled up talking about her. So can we drop it?"

"I'm just saying, she could've left it till tomorrow. And what was with those fake tears?"

Enzo didn't think it was the right time to point out they hadn't seemed fake to him. Instead, he took a breath and tried to diffuse the situation before it got out of hand. "Come on now, she's gone. Forget about it. You've got far more important things to think about. Let's focus on that instead, all right?"

Her hand immediately went up to her face again, where the thin but deep scars criss-crossed her temple and cheek. As had become habitual, she arranged the hair to cover the scars. The action tore at his heart. God, he hoped the test results came through okay.

Cara's decision to undergo plastic surgery to remove the scars had been a huge and surprising step. He hoped for her sake it succeeded. He hated to think what would happen to her emotionally if it failed. He saw the shadows under her eyes and pulled her into another quick hug.

He adored his baby sister, even though at times, in his deepest private moments, he despaired about whether he was doing right by her.

She'd been diagnosed with manic depression after their parents died when she was nineteen. Her boyfriend dumping her for her best friend soon after hadn't helped.

Adored as a child by parents who'd thought they wouldn't have any more children after Enzo, she'd been devastated when they died in an interstate pile up. Being betrayed by not only her boyfriend, but also her best friend, had dealt her a blow she'd almost not recovered from.

Overnight, she turned from a bubbly fun-loving college student to a clingy, suicidal, sophomore drop out, living in the house he shared with Roxanne, his girlfriend at the time.

Her unpredictable tantrums had eventually driven Roxanne away, and every subsequent girlfriend had run a mile, until Enzo had finally admitted he couldn't handle his sister's care on his own.

He'd convinced her to see a therapist and, in just a year, Cara had undergone an immense change, almost returning to the way she used to be. He'd even hoped she might go back to college and finish her law degree. When he'd broached the subject with the therapist, she'd suggested they get away from LA for a while instead, take a trip somewhere, give

Cara the chance to meet new people and form different relationships.

And so, what had started out as a three-week vacation to Thailand had ended up as an eighteen-month adventure around the world, ending in London, where he'd met Lexi, the woman of his dreams. *Or so he'd thought.*

Tired of living in faceless hotels, he'd suggested they rent a house for the month-long stay they'd planned in London. The last thing he'd expected when Cara had dragged him along to view the rental house her so-called Relocation Expert had found was to fall hard and fast.

He'd known how it felt to literally feel your heartstrings being plucked by love. The sensation, coupled with Lexi's amazing beauty, had left him reeling in the entry hall of the house they were viewing that long ago winter morning.

When his less-than-subtle questioning of Cara had revealed Lexi's love of salsa, the dance she indulged in every Wednesday night at a salsa bar near their hotel, he'd made sure to plant himself there the very next Wednesday. And the relief when Lexi walked in had given way to a blood-draining hard-on at the sight of her sexy dress and stunning body.

The same hard-on which had led him to foolishly propose three months later with his heart on his sleeve and high on love, mind-blowing sex, and happiness.

Only to be brought crashing down by hard reality, his dreams turned to ashes.

Never, ever again.

From now on, Cara was what mattered in his life. Nothing else.

He pulled her close. "Everything will be all right. So, what say we go and grab some early dinner? How about Mexican, your favorite? Then you can tell me more about this doctor of yours."

After a moment's hesitation, Cara nodded, her gaze softening as she looped her arm through his and recounted what the doctor's prognoses were.

But Enzo was only half-listening. A greater, crazy, part of him was wondering why he felt as if he'd let himself down by not defending Lexi more.

Chapter Seven

Déjà vu. Some believed there was no such thing. So why then did she feel as if she'd relived this moment, this day, before?

Lexi shut the door behind her, lobbed her keys onto the coffee table, and undressed as she went through her apartment to the bedroom. Again, her case stood just inside the door. She kicked off her shoes next to it.

Again, she took a shower which cleansed her, but didn't manage to completely get rid of the hospital smell.

At any moment, she expected her cell to beep a message from Enzo.

Fat chance. Besides, even if he did call, she intended to follow through with the decision she'd made on the way home from the hospital.

They couldn't go on like this. The sex was mind-blowing. But the pain that came with it was too much to bear.

It was time to end things.

But can you do that? Cut him off just like that? Cutting off her own arm would be easier, but somehow she had to find the strength to do it. Fiona was on the mend. There really was no reason to stay in L.A. She could relocate. That was her expertise after all. Vegas would be a blast. New

York even better. Or maybe she could go back home to London.

No.

London could never be home again.

Maybe she would take a sabbatical. Stay with her grandmother in Edinburgh for a few months. The month-long vacation she'd planned for her honeymoon was still owed her, as was the vacation time she'd accrued working for the last year without a break.

She couldn't go to her grandmother, though. Nana Mayfield may be old, but her sharp eyes and shrewd brain would detect her broken spirit within minutes, and the last thing she needed was to be interrogated by an expert. The need to unburden herself was far too tempting. But she couldn't do that to Nana. Her grandmother would be devastated if she knew…

The knock on the door startled her.

Not expecting anyone, she didn't plan on opening the door, especially wearing only a towel, but a look through the peephole made her jerk back. The face was distorted, but unmistakable.

Enzo? What the hell was he doing here?

She bit her lip, debated whether to ignore the knock, pretend she wasn't home--

"Forget it. I can hear you behind the door, baby. Open up."

Sucking in a sustaining breath, she opened the door a crack, but left the safety chain in place. "Wh—what're you doing here?"

His face was taut, his eyes gleaming. "You didn't answer your cell, so I came to see you instead. Let me in."

She realized she hadn't switched it on after leaving the hospital. But why would he want to contact her? Had something else happened?

"Fiona? Is she—?"

He shrugged. "She's okay as far as I know. But I didn't come here to talk about her. Look, will you just open the door?"

"Why? What do you want? And how do you know where I live?"

He glanced down the hall and back at her. "There's a lady down the hall listening to every word we're saying. So unless you want to carry on this conversation on the door step…?"

Mrs. Broadbent was a nosy divorcee who made it her business to find out everything about everyone who lived on the block. Lexi hesitated, even though a part of her knew this was a perfect opportunity to carry through her decision to end things with Enzo. But somehow she'd thought, perhaps hoped, she'd have until Friday to do so. *Maybe get one last fuck out of it first?* a sardonic voice whispered.

"Dammit, will you let me in before I kick this goddamn door down?" he growled.

She unlatched the door and stepped back, then immediately regretted her decision when Enzo's hot gaze raked over her near naked body. By the time his eyes reached her bare toes, they were both breathing hard.

"Right, I guess you not wanting to let me in makes sense now." He slowly licked his lips and Lexi was pretty sure he didn't even realize he was doing it.

"It wasn't this...that wasn't why..."

His gaze travelled back up and molten heat pooled low in her belly. "Wasn't it? Because I'm pretty sure you know what it does to me to see you looking like that."

"I...Enzo..." She took another step back, although every sense in her clamored to get closer to him. He followed, kicked the door shut and just stared at her.

A deep breath for fortitude turned into torture when his sandalwood-scented aftershave attacked her frail senses. Her hand tightened on the knot in her towel.

"The...uh...living room is through there." She pointed in the vague direction and succeeded in distracting him.

But as he looked around her condo for the first time, she began to feel even more exposed than she'd felt when he was staring at her in nothing but the towel.

This was her private space, her sanctuary. Getting him out of her life would be hard enough without having the added memory of his presence here.

The need to have him out of here as fast as possible spiked through her. But she couldn't throw him out wearing only a towel. "I—I need to get changed. I'll be right back. Take a seat."

His gaze slammed back to hers, his eyes almost burning holes through the flimsy towel. "Sure you don't want to invite me into your bedroom, baby? I could help you, uh…change." The husky temptation in his voice almost undid her.

Did she want to invite him into her bedroom?

With every single fiber of her being!

She took another step back and prayed for strength. "No, thanks. Actually, I'm glad you came. We need to talk."

His eyes shot up from their survey of her legs. "We do? What about?"

"Wait here, I'll be right back."

She flew to her room, dropping her towel on the floor. At her dresser, she extracted a pair of black briefs from her drawer and was just about to slip them on when her door banged open.

"Sorry, baby, I got tired of waiting," the low rumble of his voice was tinged with amusement since it'd barely been a minute.

Lexi jerked upright and dropped the briefs. Moss green eyes slid down her naked form, lust blazing all the way. At the juncture of her thighs, lust morphed into something else. "*Who the hell did you shave yourself for?*" he bellowed.

She swallowed at the volcanic fury in his eyes. He seemed to grow in proportion with his rage, filling her room as he charged toward her.

For you, you dolt. "For myself."

He closed in on her, seizing her arm in a painful hold. "Don't lie to me! Did you fuck someone else in Vegas? Someone who didn't want to see any hair on your perfect little mound?"

She tried to shove him away. "Piss off! I won't be spoken to like that, Enzo."

"Answer me!"

"No, I will not."

He paled. "God, you did, didn't you? It's written all over your face."

"And what if I did? Am I the only woman you've slept with since we met again?"

***

The unexpected question threw Enzo even as he reeled under the weight of fury, pain and gut-clawing jealousy. To admit he hadn't slept with another woman since she came on the scene six months ago would be to confess a deep, deadly obsession even he refused to acknowledge. But he couldn't answer in the negative. There was only one liar in this room, and it wasn't him.

"Just tell me straight. For once in your life, tell the truth. Did you get naked for someone else in Vegas?"

Her tongue flicked over her lips. "No, I didn't. Not exactly."

He jerked her closer, trying his damnedest to ignore what the softness of her warm body did to his. "What the hell does that mean? Either you did or you didn't."

"In that case, no, I didn't."

The relief he should've felt was absurdly absent. She was trying to fuck with his mind. He spiked one hand in her hair, exerting pressure to tilt her face up to his.

"I'll ask one last time. Did another man see you naked on your trip?"

She remained silent, her eyes square on his. But her color rose.

Red, the color of guilt.

"*Jesus.* You did!" He wondered why he felt so hurt. How long had he known she had a loose relationship with the truth?

"No, I didn't. I swear, I didn't have sex with anyone else."

"Then what?"

"It was nothing; just a massage."

"What kind of massage?"

"Oh, come on Enzo—!"

"*What kind?*"

"The usual kind."

"When it comes to you, baby, we both know *usual* is a whole different ballgame." His grip tightened. "Explain."

"No, I won't. You're just going to have to tr—" She stopped herself from saying the word.

"Trust you? *Trust* you? I'm sure you won't be offended if I laugh?" Although, right now laughing was the last thing he felt like doing. "Just tell me what this massage entailed."

"Look, Enzo, it was a normal massage. But if you want the whole truth, the guy who gave the massage this time was the same one who gave a…different one the last time I was there."

"You mean you fucked him? You fucked him in Vegas?" he bit out, a strange numbness spreading inside.

Her chin rose. "Yes, I did. Seven months ago," she added in a low voice.

"*Seven months*? You mean before you and I…"

She nodded.

This time relief smashed through, flooding him with a heady emotion. Instinct said she told the truth, even though the clear steady gaze that held his meant nothing.

"Then why did you shave everything off?" She knew how much he loved her pubes. There was something insanely sexy and earthy about running his fingers through her her curls before cupping her.

"I—I wanted to try it another way..."

He frowned. "What way?"

She lifted a bare, smooth shoulder in a self-conscious shrug. "I've heard the feeling's more…sensitive…down there if there's no hair." More hot color flowed up her face, and a reluctant smile tug at his lips.

"Really? That's interesting." His eyes flicked to the bed – the nice double bed with the flower-motif coverlet. "Maybe we should test the theory?"

He saw the heat he felt reflected in her eyes, and his cock grew so hard, he saw stars. Anticipatory warmth flooded his mouth, but to his surprise, she shook her head and stepped away.

"Why the hell not?" he bit out, the very idea of having to leave here without fucking her making him want to smash his fist into something. "It's not Friday, I know," his voice sounded pitiful and pleading even to his own ears. "But I'm here, you're here. You want to fuck me, and I sure as hell want you to. Seeing you today at the hospital... God, baby, I've missed you. I know you've missed me too. So what's the problem?" When he tried to back her toward the bed, she pulled away.

"You were horrible to me at the hospital."

He stopped and clawed a hand through his hair. "I know. And I'm sorry. Seeing you there was a shock. And Cara...well she's making some tough decisions right now and she needs me." He started toward her again. "I don't want to talk about that now. Hell, I don't want to talk, period."

"But I do." She grabbed a robe, shrugged it on and she moved to the window. For several seconds, Lexi stood looking at the view of the ocean before facing him. "Besides, you still haven't told me why you're here. You turned up on my doorstep unannounced. Why?"

He hesitated, because telling her he'd wanted to see if she was all right would make him sound even more lame and needy than he had a few seconds ago.

He looked at her without answering. The shadows under her eyes were still visible and the air of fragile weariness surrounded her like a cloak. Just like last Friday, he experienced an unexpected and unwelcome tug of concern.

"Why, Enzo?"

He shrugged. "I was in the neighborhood and wanted to make sure we were still meeting on Friday. When you didn't answer your phone, I thought I'd make a personal call. So, are we?"

She didn't answer, but the strange, resolved look in her eyes sent a dull thud through his heart.

"You said you wanted to talk. What the hell is it? Spit it out," he rasped forcefully when she remained silent.

A sensation close to dread crawled up his spine. If she thought she could tell him it was over, she had another think coming. If anyone was going to call off this thing between them, it would be him, not her. *God, how desperate did he sound?*

"What happened last Thursday can't happen again," she said in a sudden rush.

A red haze clouded his vision. She *was* dumping him.

"Like hell it can't! You think you can just end this thing between us? Just like that?" He ignored the hurt in her eyes, desperate to exact as much hurt as she was bent on inflicting on him. "You think anyone else can give you what I can? Tell me, when was the last time anyone made you come like I did? Made you scream from your orgasm the way I do?"

"Enzo—"

"Shut up! Shut the hell up and listen. You want to call this off? Fine. But if you walk away from me, you better keep walking. There isn't room in LA for both of us."

"That's ridiculous!"

The ice continued to freeze around his heart. "Those are the terms. We keep seeing each other or you leave LA."

"That's bollocks! You can't force me to leave town."

"You think not? Just try it and see. You forget, this is America. We're a very litigious bunch. We love to sue the crap out of each other. One, maybe two letters of complaint to your boss, the threat of litigation, and you'll be out on your ass so quick, you'll leave skid marks."

Her arms clamped around her waist, her eyes wide and haunted. "That's blackmail! Why? Why are you doing this?"

He ignored the mingled pain and confusion in her voice. In three strides, she was within reach. He pulled her resistant body to his. "Because I'm not done with you. Not by a long shot. And deep down, I know you're not done with me. You know how bad I've yearned for you since you've been away? How I've longed to feel your perfect mouth around my cock? You want to end this? You think you can walk away, not feel my cock inside you, hitting that sweet, sweet spot, ever again? Is that what you want, baby?" He breathed the words into her parted mouth and she made a jerky little sound in her throat.

He slid his hands over her ass, cupping the perfect, sexy mounds. She trembled, and her tongue darted out to lick her lower lip. His temperature kicked up a notch. Smoothing his hands up her back, he brought them round until he had the glorious weight of her breasts in his hands.

Letting loose a groan, he passed eager thumbs over her silk-covered rock hard nipples, fighting the urge to part her robe and suck on them. He couldn't. Not yet. Not until he made damn sure she wasn't about to kick him to the curb.

"Look me in the eye and tell me you can walk away from this."

She refused to meet his gaze, her half-closed eyes riveted on his mouth. Desperate, he pressed home his advantage. "You can't, can you?"

***

Lexi sucked in a shaky breath, and knew she was lost. With his hands on her body and his thick cock pressed so dominantly against her belly, she knew she couldn't--wasn't ready to--walk away from him. When he flicked her nipples again, fresh heat oozed between her thighs in a rush of surrender.

"You can't, can you?" he repeated again, triumph coating his voice and she sagged against him. But within that triumph, Lexi imagined she heard relief.

"No, I can't," she whispered, feeling that same relief echo through her.

His lips lifted in a smile before his head descended.

The kiss was hot. It blazed. It scorched. He plastered her against him and, like a starved soul given a feast, she opened herself up with all her senses. But just before she drowned in the sea of lust, a thought impinged.

She tore her mouth away, ignored his impatient growl and hungry lips, and stepped back.

"Before this goes any further, we need to clarify one thing." She took a deep steadying breath. "Whoever you were in that bedroom last week, I don't want any of it. You made me beg for you, Enzo. I don't want that. Whatever happens between us will be by mutual agreement. If you're angry, leave your anger at the door, or I'll walk. And *if* I do decide to end this thing between us, I'd thank you not to threaten me the way you just did. You may be a powerful businessman, but you don't own LA. I am my own woman. I come and go as I please. Are we clear?"

He rocked back on his heels, his fierce gaze on her face. When he didn't answer immediately, her palms dampened with dread. What if he said no? Her mind screeched with the effect that answer would have on her. How long had it taken before her brave decision to break things off had crumbled to dust? One look, one touch was all it'd taken.

She was hooked on him, pure and simple, but she forced herself to be strong. Her control had been violently taken away from her a year ago.

Hanging on to it now was as vital to her as breathing.

Finally, he nodded. "I'm sorry I threatened you. That was stupid and out of line. But are you saying that deep down, you didn't enjoy what happened last Thursday? Relinquishing your power to me, letting me take control? Did that not turn you on, even more than usual?"

His question jerked her back to awareness. It knocked about in her brain, seeking accommodation. The urge to admit the truth and say yes, she'd enjoyed it, sat at the tip of her tongue. She yearned to tell him how it had made her feel, the freedom she'd enjoyed from giving herself up to him, letting him call the shots.

A very big part of her wanted that, wanted to give herself over to him.

But that would hand him the power, something she'd vowed never to do. She'd been reduced to utter helplessness once, stripped of every ounce of her power and self-respect. After picking herself up from that horrific time in her life, she'd sworn nothing would make her relinquish her power to another human being ever again.

She looked up into Enzo's hot green eyes. "No."

Surprise and disappointment flared in his eyes, and then it disappeared. Nodding once, he said, "Fine. We'll do things your way. But I have my own stipulations. From now on, no once-a-week meeting. We see each other whenever we feel the urge."

Her pulse accelerated. "That's not what we agreed to."

"I'm changing the rules." His hands caressed her shoulders and he stepped closer, enforcing his authority with a sly thrust of his erection against her belly. "Seven days is too long. When you leave I spend the next six days in goddamn limbo, counting the seconds until I see you again."

Shock spiked through her. "You do?"

He laughed. "It's no use hiding it, sweetheart. I'm addicted to you. To your smell, your touch, the heaven I feel when I'm deep inside you. You've crawled under my skin. I can't think straight when you're not in my arms and I can't think straight when you are. Yeah, I'm a mess and sure as hell didn't know what I was thinking when I suggested a weekly meeting. That ends today."

"But how will we see each other? You work nights at your clubs. I work during the day." And then there was Cara, she added silently.

"I've hired a new manager, and my partner keeps an eye on things. Owning sixty percent of the business means I'm my own boss and can do pretty much what I want. And what I want right now is you." He bent forward and took an earlobe between his teeth as he eased her robe off. She shuddered helplessly. "So, we are agreed?"

Her skin tingled with pleasure. "All right. But not here," she rushed in. "This is non-negotiable." Only blind need drove her to allow him here today, but she couldn't take him showing up at her door whenever he pleased.

He shrugged. "Fine. We'll continue to meet at the penthouse." He stepped close and walked her backward toward the bed. "Now, we've wasted enough time. I need to fuck you now before my cock explodes from neglect."

Lifting her hand, he placed it on his fly. "Feel how hard I am for you, baby? What are you going to do about it?"

Her fingers convulsed around his thick shaft and he gave a winced groan.

Today he wore chinos, not the tight jeans she loved him in, but it gave her the advantage of gripping him firmly through the material, to stroke him the way she knew drove him wild. "Does this help?" she teased.

He moaned, pulled her closer, and sucked on a pulse in her neck. "Oh yeah, that's it, baby. Stroke me, just like that."

His hands slid over her back and down to knead her ass. A rush of air-conditioned air passed between her exposed legs. Shivers raked her body as it cooled the moisture seeping from her. One finger slid between her cleft, torturing her with pleasure.

"Damn, you're so wet. I can't wait to slide inside your tight cunt."

The back of her knees touched the bed. A small push from him and she fell back onto the covers. He took a long minute to run his gaze over her, and everywhere his gaze touched, fire followed. He paused at her mons. This time his expression grew hotter with lust, not anger.

"Hmm, maybe there's an advantage to this look, because I love seeing your pussy, wet and ready, even with your legs closed." One hand trailed over her thigh, teasing it near her now bald triangle before moving on. He lifted a knee to the bed, but before he could settle over her, she held up a hand.

He frowned.

"Equality, remember?"

A growl sounded from him. "What is it you want?"

She crossed her legs, hiding herself from him. His frown deepened. "Let's see. I'm naked, you're not."

A sexy grin slashed his face. "That's easily taken care of." He reefed his T-shirt over his head. Chinos, boxers, and shoes followed. "Better?"

Lexi reached for him and smoothed a palm over his hot, velvet-over-steel cock. "Much."

His tongue invaded her mouth as his hand closed over hers and guided her hand up and down his shaft. His tongue mimicked what he planned to do to her very soon. "Do you mind if we don't extend the foreplay past sixty seconds?" he asked urgently when they broke for air. "I need you badly."

In spite of the day she'd had--good news thrown in with knowing her chance of happy ever after with Enzo was shattered--she laughed.

Right this minute, with the man who possessed her mind and body in her arms, nothing could dampen her spirits, not even the thought that he was here just for sex. She laughed again, a husky sound that filled the sanctuary of her bedroom.

"Sixty seconds, eh? I think we can find something to do with that time. Wanna sixty-nine?"

Hot eyes gleamed down at her as he straightened. "Baby, that's so '80s. I have a better idea. Come here."

Rising from the bed, she approached him, her gaze drinking in his powerful body and erection. A feminine part of her gloried at being able to evoke such a reaction in him. When her nipples brushed his chest, he inhaled sharply. Her smile of pleasure turned into a yelp when his hands closed around her waist. Before she could blink, she was upside down. He adjusted her length so her thighs rested over his shoulders, her wet heat wide open to him.

Supporting her weight with one powerful arm clamped around her waist, he parted her with his other hand and dropped a light kiss on her flowered petal. Never before had she felt anything like this. She gasped at the wildness of it.

"Feel free to enjoy yourself down there. I fully intend to test your sensitivity up here," he said with a muffled chuckle, and passed a sleek tongue along her passage. "God, you taste so good."

An uncontrollable spasm gripped her, the blood rushing to her head increasing her pleasure.

Eager to bestow equal pleasure before she passed out from ecstasy, she gripped one taut thigh to steady herself and grasped his velvety length. Parting her lips, she took his cock in her mouth.

A hot rush of air flowed over her pussy, followed a second later by a deep moan. Then he took her nether lips delicately between his teeth, coaxed his tongue over and over her clit, and sent her wild and skating blindingly toward her inevitable orgasm.

Her frenzied sucking increased with her own pleasure. Enzo's tongue became an instrument of torture as he took her close, only to pull back at the last moment.

She refused to beg like she had last Thursday. What she did was get her own back. She took as much of him as she could, right to the back of her throat. She felt him jerk, felt his powerful thigh muscles trembled beneath her hand as he drowned in sensation.

To pay her back, he buried his tongue in her pussy. All thought flew out of her head as her hips bucked against his mouth, seeking more, dying for the final tumble into ecstasy.

With a series of flicks against her engorged clit, he sent her soaring.

Stars exploded behind her closed lids. She moaned around his cock, her tongue laving him even as her whole body bucked against his. Her convulsions seemed to take an eternity, until finally he moved forward and laid her on the bed.

Through drowsy lids, she saw him poised above her, his huge shaft and scrotum inches from her face. Raising her head, she licked the thick vein on the underside of his shaft.

"Fuck, baby!" he breathed. "That's not a good idea," he growled, but didn't move away. With one hand he traced her hot flesh from cleavage to thigh and back again. "Was that good for you?"

Barely able to speak, she rasped, "It was amazing." She whispered a finger over the vein she'd just licked. "And you lasted more than sixty seconds."

He smiled around a groan, the delicious curve of his up-side-down lips causing another wave of emotion to suffuse her. "Hmm. I decided I wanted to see your face when I come."

Her heart caught, lurched, and hammered painfully. He'd said that to her the first time they made love. *I want to look into your eyes when I come. I want to bare myself to you, let you see what you do to me.*

Nothing in his expression showed he remembered that time. He leaned down, kissed her deep and long, the taste of her orgasm on their lips.

Without breaking the kiss, he tugged on a condom. Then he shifted position and settled between her legs, his thighs spreading hers wide apart. His cock nudged her entrance. She moved restlessly beneath him, eager for the sensation only he could give her.

The skin over her hairless mound stretched when he pushed inside her.

"Open your legs wider."

She did. The feel of him as he filled her blew her mind. "Good. So good."

When he pulled his upper body from hers she began to protest, but he took her with him as he sat back on his heels so she straddled him. "Now, arch your back. See how that feels."

Again she did as he wanted. Sensation exploded through her as the skin along her neck, torso, and abdomen tightened even further, pulling her taut where it most counted.

He started to move in and out of her, each thrust filling her with his immense power. He dropped his head and took one nipple in his mouth.

She gasped, then sucked in desperate air as the pressure built inside her. "Enzo!"

Releasing her nipple, he licked along her neck to her lobe. "I'm here, baby. Right here with you."

His rocking increased; his hands on her hips controlling his thrusts. Heat shot through her. She ground her pelvis into his and felt his movements become slightly uncoordinated as sensation gripped him. She took him ever deeper inside her as he pushed them to the edge.

Lexi locked a hand on his nape and met him thrust for thrust, giving him everything she had as they rocketed toward the heavens.

He bucked hard against her, his guttural cry hot against her neck. She followed him, her spasms wild and unfettered as her orgasm tore through her. Against her chest, she felt his harsh breaths, their sweat-drenched bodies slick in the gathering darkness.

"God, you're amazing," he panted. "So fucking amazing."

Lexi smiled around the sadness in her heart. She wanted to tell him she was amazing because she was with him, but she didn't. She kissed his cheek and he lowered her to the bed. Sleep tugging at her lids, she clamped both arms around him and, with a sigh, gave in to the oblivion of sleep.

Several hours later, she woke to find him curled around her, his chest rising and falling against her back. The sensible thing to do would have been to wake him, tell him to leave so she could have her sanctuary back.

But she couldn't bear to let him go. Not yet.

Just for tonight, she let him stay.

Chapter Eight

"You're going to see Lexi, aren't you?"

Enzo tensed with a hand on the doorknob. Damn, he'd thought she was asleep. Hell, when he checked on Cara a half hour ago, she'd been out like a light. Now, he felt like a teenager caught sneaking out on a school night.

Desperation clawed at him. Lexi was avoiding him. The three weeks since they started seeing each other on a full-time basis had been great. Fantastic, in fact. Right up until these last few days.

Now, every time he suggested they meet up, she came up with some excuse not to. Tonight when he'd phoned her, she said she might have to go to New York at the last minute and she was packing. Who the hell packed for a *just in case* trip? When he'd asked her how long she'd be gone, she said she didn't know. Damned if he'd let her string him along with non-answers like that. He'd tried her cell again. It was switched off, and she wasn't answering her house phone.

Something was wrong. He refused to believe she was growing tired of him. The same way he refused to believe she was seeing someone else. No matter how well a woman could lie, Enzo couldn't believe Lexi could screw him the way she did and go off to do the same with another guy.

"Well, are you?"

He let go of the door. Turning to face Cara, he steeled himself for the confrontation.

However unfortunate the timing, the time had come to bring things out in the open.

He was tired of hiding. Lexi might no longer hold a special place in his life, but she held *a* place. Besides, he was a grown man of thirty-four, and he'd had enough of skulking around. He could damn well choose who he saw.

"What if I am?" he challenged, even as part of him wondered whether this decision was the right one. Granted, in the last couple of weeks, Cara had made amazing progress. The sample skin grafts the hospital had used on her face had done their job. The surgery was scheduled for three weeks' time. Cara seemed happy, but did he risk pushing her back into her black hole if he admitted he was seeing Lexi?

Proceed with caution.

He watched as she came to sit on the sofa and tuck her legs under her. "She's really got you hooked, hasn't she?"

Resentment burned at the statement, but he ignored it. The larger part of him waited for her to freak out, the way she always did. "No one's got me hooked. And I didn't say I was going to see her." *Chicken.*

"Don't take me for a fool, big brother. I saw the way you looked at her the other day at the hospital. Now, you always leave the room when your cell rings. And yes, call me sneaky, but I checked your phone. Unless you've got a girlfriend with the initial L who texts you those hot messages, I'm guessing L stands for Lexi."

He clenched a fist, tensing for the histrionics which were sure to come. But his sister remained on the sofa, her demeanor calm, even relaxed. What was going on here?

"I should chew you out for going through my personal stuff without permission. But for argument sake, if L happens to be Lexi, would you have a problem with that?"

"Yes, I would."

Enzo's heart plummeted, but he refused to let her answer sway him. He sat opposite her and he took a deep breath.

"Cara, I think it's time we had a talk. I've been here for you for the last year, hell, for the last twenty-three years. And I'll continue to be here for you no matter what. But you have to let me live my life. Whether I'm seeing Lexi or not should not come between us. I know what she did caused you a lot of pain, but you need to move on. I think you have, in fact, which is why you're so calm right now. This doesn't have to come between us unless you let it."

His sister tilted her head to one side, regarding him with solemn eyes. "You still love her, don't you?"

"*What?*" His harsh laugh sounded hollow in his ears, and this time when his heart plummeted, it went farther down.

"You still love her." A statement this time, said with a certainty that sent cold dread through him.

He gave a sharp shake of his head. "No, I don't love her. But there's unfinished business between us."

"And you don't wonder why, after all this time, it's still unfinished? Are you sure you'll ever finish it? Do you even *want* to finish it? You talk to me about moving on. How have you moved on in the last year? As far as I know, you haven't dated anyone or had so much as had a one-night stand since Lexi came to LA. Okay, so I admit I'm not proud of how I've behaved, and I know I've been more than a handful for you." She held up a hand. "No, don't say anything to make me feel better. I know I've been a superbitch this last year. What's *your* excuse?"

He smiled after he winced. "For being a superbitch?"

She didn't return his smile.

He shook his head again. "We're not talking about me; and you've had good reasons to react the way you did."

She smiled at him, a small grateful smile. "All the same, it took me too long to realize just what I was doing. I just—I just hope I've woken up in time to stop hurting the people who care about me."

"And Lexi? You going to make things right with her too?"

He immediately regretted pushing her when her expressive face closed up. What the hell was he doing, asking for absolution for the person who'd caused of all their misery?

Surely, he wasn't thinking of forgiving her himself?

Something shifted inside him.

Hadn't Lexi paid enough? Shouldn't she also be allowed to move on with her life? *But that means you have to let her go.*

He ruthlessly ignored the voice in his head and held up a placatory hand to his sister. "Maybe not just yet. But think about it. It could be the last positive step to putting all this behind you."

"Well, that a little tough to do," she indicated her face, "when I see this every time I look in the mirror."

"If you sort out the emotional side, by the time the physical side is fixed, you'll be whole again. Think about it." He got up, went over, and kissed her on the forehead. "Try and get some sleep."

"Hmm. I might do that. I don't want to go on my date looking like a scarecrow."

He paused on his way to the door. "Date?"

Cara stood up, a smile lifting her lips. "Yep. I'll tell you all about it in the morning. You didn't answer my question. Are you going to see Lexi?"

After a moment's thought, he shook his head. "No, I think I'll head over to the night club and put in a few hours' work before Larry throws another tantrum."

He tried to decipher the look that came over her face, but failed when her face cleared and she smiled. "Okay, Goodnight, big bro."

"Goodnight, lil sis."

He'd give Lexi a night to stew in whatever was bothering her, give her a chance to work it out of her system. Then if she didn't call him by tomorrow, he'd find her, sit her down for a talk.

Things were about to change between them. It was time to take this...whatever this thing was between them to another level.

This time when he grasped the doorknob, his heart was a whole lot lighter.

***

Lexi zipped her case and put her suit bag on top. Her hints about going to New York to scope things out there had finally paid off and her trip looked like a certainty now. What her boss didn't know was that she planned to use the trip to find an apartment for herself.

Enzo was right after all. LA wasn't big enough for both of them.

Pain ripped at her heart, the way it always did when thoughts of never seeing him again encroached. With her departure was almost a reality, the very sight of him made her feel as if she had a gaping hole in her chest.

She couldn't live like this any longer.

She loved him. She'd never stopped. But he didn't love her. Simple as that.

It was all about the sex for him. She knew that. But it hurt knowing that it was the first and last thing he wanted every time they met up.

Sure, in the last weeks they'd thrown in things like a dinner at an Italian restaurant Enzo loved and the odd movie, even a baseball game. But he made it evident in every look, every gesture, that he couldn't wait to get back to the penthouse and fuck her.

The sex was great – hell, it was beyond great - but whoever said it was better to have loved and lost than to never have loved was a moron. Her heart bled every time she walked away from him; every time he shot her that heated look and tried to arrange another sexual marathon with her; every time he gasped *baby* instead of her name when they made love, her heart shredded a little bit more.

She checked her handbag for the passport she always carried in case her clients' requests changed. The client who wanted a place in New York would be calling within the next forty-eight hours, but she prayed the call would come sooner. She had a feeling Enzo suspected something was up with her. Avoiding his calls wouldn't work for much longer. The quicker she got away from him the better. If he turned up at her condo, she wouldn't open up. Simple.

The doorbell jangled, as if conjured up by her imagination. Her breath clogged in her throat. Forcing herself to remain where she was, she prayed he'd go away. The second ring was longer, more insistent.

Sweat coated her palms. *Please, please, go away.* Silence greeted her unspoken plea. After several minutes, she allowed herself a sigh of relief. Moving down the hallway to the kitchen, she put the kettle on. Chamomile tea would calm her shot nerves.

The mug she'd plucked from cupboard fell and shattered when a bold fist hammered on the door.

Leaving the shards of her favorite cup on the floor, she marched to the door, and wrenched it open.

"In case you didn't get the message, Enzo, I don't want to—" Her words dried up in her throat when she saw who stood on her threshold. "Cara!"

"Hi, Lexi. May I come in?" Her gaze reflected her nerves as she fiddled with her purse strap.

"I—what are you doing here?"

Black eyebrows quirked. "I almost gave up until your neighbor told me you were in. Do I need to beg to be invited in?" There was a hint of anxiety in her voice.

Lexi's shock gave way to trepidation when she spied a hint of challenge in Cara's eyes. The last thing she needed was another confrontation. But instinct told her to take it easy.

She stepped back. "Sure…umm, come in."

Cara walked in, removing the bag slung over her shoulder as she looked around. "From your reaction, I take it Enzo didn't come here?"

Lexi fought to hide her surprise. "Why would your brother come here?"

Cara didn't answer. Instead, she dumped her bag on the coffee table. "Nice place. I like the view." Her boots clacked on the hardwood floor as she strolled to the window.

Not sure how to take this, Lexi shut the door and remained where she stood. "Err, thanks. Can I get you something to drink? I was just about to make myself some tea."

Her visitor swung round, the folds of her asymmetrical top flaring over her jeans as she turned. "Tea?" She wrinkled her nose. "No thanks. I'll take something stronger if you've got it."

"I don't, I'm afraid. I…I don't drink anymore."

A strange look crossed over Cara's face. "Water's fine then, thanks." She rubbed her hands over her thighs in a gesture at odds with her normally confident self.

Lexi's trepidation increased as she went into her small kitchen. Why would Cara think Enzo was here? Had he told his sister about them?

Side stepping the broken porcelain on the floor, she grabbed glasses and two bottles of mineral water from the fridge and returned to the living room.

Cara had taken a seat on the large sofa. Opening her bottle, Lexi poured the drink and placed it in front of her. She didn't touch her own water, too scared of choking if she tried to take a sip.

"So, what—"

"I'm sorry—"

They stared at each other, Lexi certain the gaping surprise she saw on Cara's face was reflected on her own. Cara got her emotions under control first.

"I'm sorry, Lexi," she repeated. She heaved a deep breath and released it, as if satisfied the words had come out. "For the way I've treated you this last year, for being such a bitch to you. But especially for forcing you to make that promise never to see my brother again."

Cara's words had held her rigid but the last apology made her skin crawl with shame. "I—I..."

"I know about you and Enzo."

For the second time in less than a minute, her mouth dropped open. "You do?"

"Yes. I've suspected for some time. I asked him about it tonight. He didn't admit it, but he didn't deny it either."

"I'm sorry, Cara. I tried, but I couldn't walk away from him."

The younger woman shook her head. "I had no right to ask in the first place."

"Yes, you did. Look what I did to you."

Cara's hand rose halfway to her face, but then dropped back down again. "It was an accident, Lexi. It's taken me a long time to accept that. But it was a horrible, terrible *accident*. And I've been wrong to blame you for it."

"But if I hadn't taken that drink—"

"I think I may have been to blame for that too. Maybe if I hadn't riled you so much..."

"Forget it. It wasn't that bad."

"Oh come on, I wasn't that drunk. I was a bitch because I was jealous and afraid you were taking my brother from me. I knew I upset you. Then I started at you with that truth or dare stuff. I got too personal, and I should've stopped when I saw you quietly freaking out."

"Well, you did stop."

"Obviously not quickly enough to keep you from swallowing a mouthful of that triple strength cocktail—"

Lexi's hand flew to her mouth. "Oh my God, did you say *triple* strength?"

Cara paled. "You didn't know?"

She shook her head.

Cara closed her eyes. "Oh God. Oh Shit." When she opened then again, fresh contrition blazed in their brown depths. "We suspected the bartender was watering down our drinks. That's why I went to the bar myself the last time, so I could watch him. When I complained, he added a couple extra shots for free. I just wanted us to have fun. I guess I did *that.*"

Lexi rose and went to sit next to her, relief that they were talking at last, and renewed pain at the tragedy they'd endured roiling through her. "No, please don't blame yourself. No matter what I was feeling, I shouldn't have drank that night. And when I did, I should've made us take a taxi. But I just wanted—" She stopped, unable to continue.

"You wanted to get back to see my brother?"

More pain ripped through her. She nodded, unable to hide the truth. "I was in a hurry. It made me reckless, careless. Maybe if I hadn't drank, I'd have reacted quicker." Tears gathered in her eyes. "*I'm so, so sorry, Cara.*"

Cara put her hand over hers and, when Lexi looked up, she also had tears in her eyes. "So am I," she whispered. "Enzo told me tonight that I need to move on."

Shockwaves careened through her again. "He did?"

She nodded. "We had a long talk this evening. He told me that I needed to move on to heal. I knew to do that I needed to ask your forgiveness."

"Believe me, there's nothing to forgive. Please. I should be asking for yours."

"But the way I treated you, the promise I had no right asking you to keep."

"I didn't keep it, which shows how hopeless I am."

A tremulous smile whispered over Cara's lips. "I'm glad you didn't. I think in a way, you helped my brother be strong for me."

Sadness engulfed her. "I seriously doubt that."

Cara shook her head. "The way you two feel about each other, I'm beginning to think nothing can ever come between you."

Lexi wanted to tell her the only thing her brother felt for her was molten hot lust and an unquenchable well of desire which he felt obliged to tap into regularly. But even she knew nothing lasted forever. And sizzling hot sex by its very nature, would cool with time after which they would need other tools to make any relationship between them work. Tools they did not possess. Which meant, was was between them was doomed for inevitable failure.

Only she didn't plan on being around to see it.

She put her feelings aside to hear Cara continue. "I hope I find a love like that someday."

"I'm sure you will." She tried to keep the bitterness out of her voice. It was better to let Cara believe Enzo loved her back. She couldn't deal with the pity, or worse, the assurance Cara might give that Enzo returned her feelings. Lexi knew he didn't, but the way she felt right now, any hope, even false hope, held a powerful attraction that could prove fatal to her emotions if she let her guard down.

Cara swiped a tear from her eye and pasted on a smile. "I fully intend to work on it."

Something about the way she said it made Lexi pause. "You're seeing someone?"

She gave an excited nod. "The doctor who's going to fix my face. I think he's got the hots for me."

"You mean the one in the elevator?"

"Yep. He asked me out, on a platonic basis, of course. We can't see each other while I'm his patient, but who knows what will happen after my operation. Anyway, I accepted. Fiona thinks he's hot and I should go for it."

A mixture of relief, surprise, and jealousy burned within Lexi. "I think you should, too. He seems really nice."

"You think so?"

Glad they'd moved on from the distressing conversation, she nodded eagerly. "Definitely. I think you two will be great together."

"Thanks."

They sat in awkward silence for a minute, and then Cara jumped up. "I better get back. Enzo thinks I'm in bed. Don't want him to return to find me gone. He'll go nutty."

"He's protective because he cares about you."

A sad look crossed her face. "I know. And I *have* given him reason to think he needs to take care of me. But I'm working on that. Hopefully, he'll realize he doesn't have to baby-sit me anymore." She stood up, snatched up her bag, and headed for the door. "Umm, you haven't been avoiding him by any chance, have you?"

Lexi's heart missed a beat. "What makes you say that?"

"I heard him leaving a message for you earlier. He sounded a little crazy desperate."

Lexi tried to laugh it off, but it sounded false in her own ears. "I've just been busy, that's all."

Luckily, Cara didn't pursue the matter. "Okay. Do you want to grab a coffee sometime? Maybe we can go see Fiona together this week?"

"Sure. I'd like that." She followed her to the door. "Take care of yourself, Cara. And I wish you all the best for the future."

Cara frowned. "That sounds like you're saying goodbye or something."

She cursed silently. "I'm not. I just meant for the surgery. I hope it all goes well."

"Oh, yes. Thanks, Lexi." She hovered on the doorstep as if she wanted to say something else. "See you around," she finally said.

"Bye, Cara."

With leaden feet, she went into the living room. Sinking down onto the sofa, she stared into space, silent tears streaming down her cheeks.

At last, she'd cleared the air with Cara. But any relief or joy she'd anticipated remained elusive. Like when Fiona regained consciousness, she realized she'd relied on what the effect her reconciliation with Cara would have on her relationship with Enzo. So he'd told his sister about them. Big deal. What had she expected? That he'd rush to her condo and tell her they could be a proper item now? Declare his open and undying love for her now Cara knew about them and they didn't have to hide any more?

She choked down another sob before it could emerge. From what Cara said, he'd only done it to help his sister move on with her life. Like always, his precious sister came before everyone else.

With her, it was *still* all about the sex, nothing else.

She needed to remember that and stop foolishly hoping. Swiping a shaky hand across her eyes, she picked up the glasses and bottles and took them into the kitchen.

A sob escaped her when she saw the shattered glass on the floor.

That was how she felt – broken beyond repair.

Chapter Nine

Fiona reclined, propped up against pillows, with the late afternoon sun on her closed eyelids. At first, Lexi thought she was asleep, but at the sound of the door shutting, she blinked awake.

A smile lit up her pale face. "Hey, this is a lovely surprise. I didn't know you'd be stopping by today." After almost a year of disuse, her voice sounded scratchy. In contrast, her blonde hair looked freshly shampooed and healthy.

Lexi bit her lip and tried to maintain the smile on her face. "I know. But I was in the neighborhood and thought I'd see how you were."

She berated herself for the half-lie.

After giving in to an hour-long crying jag last night, she'd dragged herself to bed and endured a sleepless night. She'd woken up this morning with a thumping headache and a firm decision. Whether she got the New York assignment or not, she had to leave LA. It was time to move on.

But before she did, she needed to say goodbye to Fiona.

Fiona gestured to her bed with a grimace. "As you can see, I'm still bound to this thing. I'm not even allowed outside to see what the world looks like after a year." Her gaze flew to Lexi's. "And don't you start crying or apologizing again!

I've had enough of that from you already. I may not remember anything after we left the nightclub that night, but I know you wouldn't have risked our lives deliberately. Shit, why am I telling you all this again?" Frustration tinged her voice.

Guilt gnawed at Lexi, but she curbed the need to ask her friend's forgiveness one last time. "Anything I can do to make you feel better?" she asked instead.

"That depends. Do you have any makeup in that bag of yours? I mean proper makeup, not lame-assed lip-gloss. I could do with, like, a serious makeover. There's a male nurse I've got my eye on."

"Fiona!" Surprised laughter erupted from Lexi.

In the three weeks since waking, Fiona had continued to surprise her. If Lexi had expected the younger woman to be despondent about being in a coma for almost a year, she'd been disappointed. Fiona had reacted as if she'd merely taken a long nap and constantly demanded to go home. Her doctor and parents had their hands full devising ways to keep her in hospital until all the requisite tests were done.

"What? I've faced death and survived it, and missed out on a year's worth of sex. So pardon me if I want to make up for it, pun intended." She sighed, then sobered. "I just want to live what's left of my life. And if I can't go home yet, if I have to stay in this godforsaken place, then I want the eye candy to appreciate me. What's wrong with that?"

"Nothing, I guess." Everyone had their own means of dealing with trauma. If this "seize life" attitude was Fiona's way of coping, who was she to argue? She pulled her bag off her shoulder and opened it. "What look were you thinking of?"

"I suppose sexy slut's out of the question," she laughed. "Okay, let's aim for, I-may-look-fragile-but-I-can-still-give-you-a-semi!"

Laughing, Lexi perched on the side of the bed. Fifteen minutes later, she stepped back. "What d'you think?"

Fiona took the mirror off the bedside stand and studied herself. "Hmm, not bad. I like that lipstick. Think I can convince Nurse Hottie to jump into bed with me when he brings me dinner tonight?"

"Without a shadow of a doubt."

Her blue eyes lit up. "Spoken like a true friend." She put the mirror down. "Now, you wanna tell me why you're really here?"

Feigning innocence crossed her mind, but she decided against it. Fiona deserved better than that. "I came to say goodbye. I'm leaving LA."

She nodded, as if she'd somehow suspected it. "Right. Cara succeeded in running you outta town, huh?"

Lexi gasped. "What? No—"

Fiona waved a feeble hand at her. "No need to pretend with me. We both know Cara. As much as I love her, she can be a selfish bitch sometimes. I have a feeling she's made your life hell these past months. My parents told me you two never visited me together; I'm not even gonna ask what that was all about, although I can guess. Look, I feel sorry for what's happened to her, to all of us, but that doesn't give her the right to dictate your life. If you don't tell her to fuck off, I—"

"You're wrong. Cara's not the reason I'm leaving. I—she came to see me and we talked, settled some things. We're okay now."

Fiona raised freshly plucked brows. "Then why…? Ah, it's the *other* Saldana."

For someone who'd been in a coma for so long, Fiona seemed exceptionally sharp. "Yes," she responded.

"Leaving town seems so drastic, not to mention melodramatic. Can't you save yourself a shit-load of shipping money and air-fare and talk to him, like you did Cara?"

"No. I get the feeling talking is the last thing on Enzo's mind."

Fiona pursed her lips and flicked an impatient hand through her hair. "Damn! I guess when it comes to thinking with their cocks nothing's changed in the past year, huh? I couldn't believe it when Cara told me he called off your engagement. You two were so crazy about each other. But I still think leaving town sends the wrong message.

"If I were you, I'd stay, find another guy, and rub what you could've had in Enzo's face. That'll set his thinking straight."

For a brief moment, Lexi's thoughts strayed to Hans, who had called her out of the blue last week to say he'd arrived in town, as promised. But as she'd decided in Vegas, hooking up with the hunky Swede wouldn't be the right thing to do.

"I mean it," Fiona stressed. "I know some hot guys. I can set you up, just say the word." Glimpses of the *femme fatale* Fiona had been before the accident broke through. Lexi was happy to see the old Fiona back out but there was no way she could do as she suggested.

She shook her head. "I can't. I'd lose my self-respect if I stay, not to mention risk a broken heart." Although, it was probably too late for the broken heart part.

"You still love him, don't you?"

She's chest tightened with pain. "I never stopped."

Fiona regarded for several seconds, and then sighed. "I hate the thought of you leaving, Lexi. But if you must, you must." She held out both hands. "Keep in touch?"

Lexi smiled and grasped the pale hands. "Of course I will. And you take care of yourself too, okay?"

Fiona rolled her eyes. "If they ever get round to letting me outta this dump, I'll take care of myself like there's no tomorrow. Count on it."

***

Once again, he'd been unable to reach her. Frustrated, Enzo thumped a fist on his steering wheel as he parked in his allotted slot outside his apartment and yanked the key out of the ignition.

On his return from the club in the early hours, he'd decided to catch a few winks before tracking Lexi down. He hadn't planned on staying out all night, but one of his barmen hadn't turned up for work and, as part owner, he'd had no choice but to step in to help. After a quick shower mid-morning, he'd rung Lexi. When her number kept going to voicemail, he'd driven to her work, only to be told she was out for the day.

Great. He slammed the door and stalked to the elevator. Now he had to wait until tonight to reach her. But reach her he would, even if he had to camp outside her condo until she came home. He'd had enough of this fucking cat-and-mouse game.

Tonight, they were sitting down to do some serious talking. It helped that Cara had chosen to sort things out between them and end her animosity toward Lexi. Now they could discuss *their* relationship. He wanted her back, full time. He wanted her to belong to him again. It wouldn't be easy – they'd have to work damned hard on the trust thing – but he wasn't ready to give up. He needed to hear what she had to say about that.

He entered his apartment, intent on digging out a cold beer to drown his frustration.

Cara, huddled on the sofa, her pale and tear-stained face twisted in pain wiped his mind clean of all else.

In two strides, he was at her side. "Cara? What's wrong? What's happened?"

"I got a call," she whispered, her voice small and broken.

"A call? Who from? Is it Fiona?" Damn, he hoped nothing bad had happened to her.

She shook her head.

"Dr. Hopkirk? Did something happen with the tests?"

"No."

"Then what the hell is it?" He tried to keep his voice level, afraid of upsetting her further, even though everything inside him wanted to scream at her to tell him. She took a deep shaky breath.

"Ian. Ian called."

"*Ian*? Pulbrook?" Disbelief followed by anger unfurled in his gut and began to spread. "What's he doing calling you? The asshole broke off your engagement when you were still in hospital. What the hell did he want?"

His sister's bitter laugh screeched along his nerves. "He said he was in town and wanted to catch up."

A tight knot seized the back of his neck. "He's here? In LA?"

She gave a stiff nod.

"How long has he been in town?"

"About a week, I think."

An uneasy feeling crept up his spine. "I hope you told him to get lost."

"Of course I did."

"Good. He won't bother you again, I'll make damn sure of it. Don't upset yourself. He's not worth it."

She picked at the sleeve of her top. "He…he apologized for the pain he caused me."

"I'm sure you told him to shove it. That slimeball isn't worth a second thought. Just put him out of your head, all right?"

Again a small nod. She opened her mouth, as if to say more.

He frowned. "What? Did he say anything else?"

"He wanted to know where Lexi lived."

A red haze washed over his eyes. He cautioned himself not to lose it. "And did you tell him?"

"No, but he asked for her phone number. I—I gave it to him. He said he wanted to catch up, for old times' sake. Maybe he wants to apologize to her, too." Fresh tears clouded her eyes.

Somehow Enzo doubted that. He wanted to demand a word-by-word replay of the conversation, but forced himself to calm down.

"Did he say where he was staying? Why he was in town?"

"He's staying at The Wiltshire, I think. As to what he's doing in LA," she shrugged, "I presume he's shooting another movie. I didn't ask him how long he was in town for." She looked up at him. "Why all these questions?"

"Nothing. Listen, I need to go out for a while. Will you be all right?"

She sniffed. "Yes, but you just got home and I cooked."

"Rain check. Call Hopkirk, I'm sure he'll jump at the chance to sample your cooking." He forced himself to smile as he backed toward the door.

Less than a minute later, he was back in his car. He forced himself to drive within the speed limit. No point risking a speeding ticket before he'd reached his destination.

After he found out what the fuck Pulbrook meant by getting in touch with his sister, and what he intended to do with Lexi's phone number, he didn't give a damn if he got arrested then. He probably would be anyway after he rearranged the son of a bitch's face for daring to encroach on what belong to him. Again.

He screeched to a stop in front of the hotel, threw his keys to the valet and strode into the lobby. Scanning the faces of the four receptionists behind the desk, he approached the bottle blonde, his most charming smile in place.

"Hi, I have an appointment with Ian Pulbrook. Can you tell me what room he's in?"

Her return smile slipped into a frown. "You have an appointment with Mr. Pulbrook? Are you sure?"

Shit. "Of course. Is there a problem?" He struggled to keep his easy stance.

"Well, yes and no. Mr. Pulbrook *is* staying here, but he's currently location-scouting."

"Really? Maybe my PA got the dates wrong. So when will he be back? I'd like to reschedule."

"We're expecting him back on Wednesday."

"Thanks, you've been a great help."

"No problem. Here, take my card. If I can be of further assistance, just give me a call."

The "I'm available" smile barely registered as he took the card.

He started to walk away. A thought occurred to him and he turned back. "How long is he in town for? Just in case, you know, our schedules clash this time round."

She smiled again and tapped a few keys on the computer. "His reservation is for three months."

He managed a nod as he backed away. By the time he reached his car, anger had taken control of him. *Three months*. What the fuck was the bastard playing at?

Did Lexi know he was in town? Had she already planned to meet up with him? Was that the reason she'd been giving him the brush off the past few days? The need to know burned through him. He was fifteen minutes away from her place.

He made it in twelve. The doorman let him in without fuss. Taking the stairs three at a time, he stalked to her door and leaned on the bell.

She opened it, her face creased in irritation. And trepidation.

"What are you doing here?"

"You mean why have I turned up on your doorstep after you've been giving me the run around all week?" He stormed past her and slammed the door. Before she could respond, he rounded on her. "Have you seen him? Is he why you're avoiding me?"

Her frown intensified. "Who are you talking about? Have I seen who?"

"Don't play games with me. Cara told me Pulbrook's been in town for a week. I'm sure he's contacted you by now."

The blood drained from her face and, for a second, he thought she'd pass out. "*Pulbrook?* Ian's in town?" she whispered.

She obviously didn't like being found out. Well, the truth had a nasty way of coming out when least expected.

"And he called Cara? Why did he do that?"

He barely heard the question through her stiff lips.

"Under some clap-trap guise of apologizing for dumping her, but we both know that's not true, don't we?"

"What?"

"I think it's interesting he ended the call by asking for your number. But you know all this because he's the reason you've been blowing me off, isn't it? Hell, he could already be here for all I know." The very idea made him want to punch something. He checked for signs of male occupancy anyway.

"Of course he isn't!"

He was sure he imagined the shudder that shook her body.

"I'm warning you, Lexi, stay away from him. I don't want anything to set back the progress Cara's made, you understand?"

She gave a short, strangled laugh. "God, that's the first time you've called me Lexi."

Confusion clouded his brain. "What?"

"It's the first time you've said my name in over a year."

He frowned. "That's bullshit." When she remained silent, he shrugged. "So what? What's that got to do with anything?"

She clasped her elbows. "Nothing. Nothing at all. Is that why you came here tonight? To warn me about seeing Ian?"

"Why else? Cara says she's fine with it, but it could all be a front. This is the last thing she needs." He watched her walk past him to sit on the sofa. She curled herself into a ball. A spurt of concern pierced his anger. "Are you all right?"

"I told you, I wasn't feeling too well."

"That was your excuse a couple of days ago; that and packing for New York." He couldn't keep the censure from his tone.

"Well, it's the truth; I've got a headache. A real one."

He stopped pacing and moved closer. She looked very pale, her eyes shadowed and large in her face. He placed a hand on her forehead. She was burning up. "Shit! When did you start feeling like this? Have you taken anything?"

"A couple of pills an hour ago. I just need to get some sleep. I'll be fine."

The anger instantly drained out of him. Bending down, he picked her up. She weighed less than he remembered. What the hell had she been doing to herself?

"Wh-where are you taking me?" she asked in a feeble voice.

"You should be in bed."

She tried to wriggle out of his arms. "No. Put me down, Enzo, I'm not in the mood."

He stopped in the hallway. "You think I want to have sex? *Now?*"

Heat crept up her face. "Well, I thought…"

"You thought wrong."

"Oh." Her voice emerged frail, weary. His chest tightened.

"Yeah, oh."

He continued walking until he reached her bedroom. He laid her on the bed, pulled the covers over her, and straightened up. Suddenly, he felt useless. "Do you need anything? A drink of water?"

Her eyes had started to droop. "No, thanks."

"Fine. Get some sleep." He started toward the door.

***

"Are you leaving?" Lexi half-hoped he would--the half that wanted time to absorb what he'd just told her. But the other half hoped he'd crawl into bed with her, hold her, and keep her safe and warm. Stop the cold spreading through her, turning her to ice.

"Do you want me to?" he asked, returning to sink down onto the side of the bed, his gaze fixed on hers.

She'd missed him so much these last few days, but she had to be strong. Very soon, she'd have to live without him. Not that she ever lived *with* him. "If you want. I'll be fine." Tiredness descended on her with a vengeance.

A shadow crossed his face. "Yeah, you said." He rose, raking a hand through his hair. He bristled with barely suppressed tension.

"Is there something else on your mind?"

He whirled around. "What?"

"You seem…agitated." Talking became an effort when blackness clawed at her. The past few nights had been hell. Now this. At least Enzo's news solved the puzzle of the silent phone calls she'd been receiving the past few days. Another shudder raked through her. She was certain Ian was her caller, even though the caller ID was blocked. Now he had her cell phone number. She'd have to change it. Again.

"It doesn't matter. Go to sleep. We'll talk when you wake up."

She wanted to ask what he needed to talk to her about, but her head thumped too hard.

"Enzo?"

"Yes?"

"I haven't seen him. Ian, I mean."

His shoulders slumped as some of the tension left him.

"Okay."

Her eyes grew heavier, her thoughts became disjointed. Staying awake hurt, looking at Enzo's beautiful face hurt even more, but anything, *anything* was better than thinking about Ian Pulbrook and what he'd done to her.

So she closed her eyes and let everything melt away.

***

Enzo looked down at her sleeping form. God, she was so fucking beautiful; if a little pale and worn around the edges. What had she been doing to herself since he last saw her?

Dark shadows lurked under her eyes and delicate veins criss-crossed her lowered lids. Her mouth had lost its pinched look, as if in sleep she'd let go of whatever troubled her. He pulled the covers higher over her and made sure her window was shut against the late afternoon breeze.

He glanced at the fragile-looking chair at the foot of her bed. No way would it take a man his size without breaking. His gaze touched longingly on the empty space beside her, but shook his head against the idea. Taking care of her was one thing. Taking care of her while *in bed* with her was something else altogether. Even sick, the sight of her body made his loins burn, so close bodily contact was out of the question until she recovered from whatever was wrong with her.

If he was to believe her – and he felt surprisingly inclined to – she'd been as surprised at the mention of Pulbrook's name as he'd been. Which meant the reason she'd avoided him had nothing to do with the asshole.

So what the hell was going on?

Had she grown tired of him? He stepped back from her, fighting the urge to kiss her awake and demand to know why she'd been freezing him out.

With a final glance at her, he started to back out of the room.

Chicken soup. His mother had always sworn by it. He might not make it how she used to, but he could put together a passable one. He could have it ready when Lexi woke up. Yeah, he'd mellow her with his chicken soup.

Or you can mellow her with sex.

Yeah, that too. He wasn't going to discount any weapon in his arsenal. But the sex would have to wait until she was better.

He grasped the doorknob, ready to shut it when he spied the cards on her dresser. He went over and plucked one from the shiny surface.

Happy thirtieth birthday.

He froze.

Dammit!

Her birthday had come and gone without even registering with him. Or had he blocked it out deliberately because he hadn't wanted to remember how they'd spent her last birthday – champagne, her favorite truffle chocolates, sex, sex, and more sex with a million *I love yous* thrown in? Casting his mind back, he tried to remember the day of her birthday. Wednesday. They hadn't met that day.

How had she spent the day? Alone? With friends? Hell, did she even have any friends in LA? Shame engulfed him. Since they met up again, he'd only wanted one thing from her. The rest of her life had not mattered to him.

Until now.

He glanced over at her and resisted another urge to wake her. He'd been so busy getting his pound of flesh, so to speak, that he hadn't stopped to take in the small details. Another card was from her grandmother. The suffer-no-fools, yet lovable old lady who would've been *his* grandmother, his family, if he'd married Lexi. Regret settled deep, touching a dark part of him he thought he'd buried.

The other cards were from her boss and a group signed card from her coworkers. Unless she'd disposed of any others, she'd received a total of four cards for her birthday.

Placing them back on her dresser, he shut the door behind him. He'd tried to tell himself he didn't really care, but he knew it was a lie. Somehow, he'd have to make it up to her.

He pulled his phone from his pocket. As he yanked open the fridge, he punched in his sister's cell number. She answered on the third ring.

"You okay?"

"Sure. Don's coming over for dinner. He'll be here shortly."

"That's great. Listen, I need ideas for a birthday present."

"Who for?"

"Who do you think?"

She laughed. "She's *your* girlfriend. Why are you asking me?"

Technically, Lexi wasn't his girlfriend, not yet, but he intended to remedy that. Soon. "Look, are you going to help me or not?"

"Fine! What were you thinking of? Big and splashy, or small and fabulous?"

He shrugged, even though she couldn't see him, and pulled open the vegetable drawer. The contents made him grimace. "I was thinking maybe a fancy dinner, or maybe I could take her shopping, you know, do that personal shopping thing you like so much. Or hey, she likes spas, right? Maybe I can book her a weekend spa package in the city somewhere."

"Lame, lame, and lame."

He straightened and shut the fridge door. The chicken soup would have to be ordered from *Paolo's*, his favorite bistro. "What d'you mean lame? I didn't see you complaining when I ordered the personal shoe shopper for your birthday."

"That's because you're my brother. But I wouldn't expect my boyfriend to buy me shoes for my birthday," she huffed. "That's what I do with my girlfriends."

"Fine, then what do you suggest?" His patience was beginning to wear thin. Maybe his sister was the wrong person to ask. He could ask Fiona—

"Well, if you really love her—"

His heart lurched. "Whoa there, I don't recall using the—er, that word at any point in this conversation."

"No, because you like to live in denial. Okay, if you *care about* her, find out what she wants and give it to her."

"Would you just stop being so damned cryptic and just tell me what you mean? Do you mean like naming a star after her or some such crap?"

Enzo gritted his teeth when she snorted in his ear. Why had he called her? He could just have gone to the mall and picked out a nice perfume or a spa basket or something.

"Now you're going beyond lame."

"Fuck it! Then what? Hey wait, she's a realtor right? Maybe I could get an architect to design her dream house." *Or what would've been our dream house.* The stab of pain came out of nowhere. He froze.

He heard a gasp followed by shocked silence.

"Wow, that's not bad, brother. Not bad at all. I'm actually quite impressed."

"Nah, scratch that idea. Besides, it's obvious you're not impressed enough, huh?"

"Well, that *is* what you'd do for the woman you loved. But seeing as you say you *don't* love her, I was thinking more of a life long *secret* wish?"

"What're you talking about?"

Five minutes later, Enzo hung up, a lot stunned and very much intrigued.

Chapter Ten

Lexi smoothed her hands down the satin material of her boy-shorts and tried to calm her jumpy nerves. Enzo would be here in five minutes. Dress sexy – that's all he'd said. So she'd worn fishnet tights and shorts with a red waistcoat over a sheer mesh top – no bra – and now she wondered whether she'd taken a blind turn at sexy and strayed into slutty-ville.

The doorbell chimed. She tugged on the hem of the shorts, then gave up. Too late to change now. The heels of her red stilettos clacked on her floorboards as she went to the intercom. "I'll be right down."

Once again, she'd let Enzo slip past the guard she'd *intended* to place around her emotions. But what sane woman could resist a man who'd nursed her back to health with homemade chicken soup, albeit homemade in *Paolo's* kitchen, glorious bubble baths, and just yesterday, a full body massage that *hadn't* ended with sex.

She'd been surprised to find him still in her apartment when she woke on Monday. Even more surprised to see him occupying her dainty antique chair, fast asleep, an abandoned health magazine propped open on his chest.

When a quick glance had shown it to be just past midnight, her surprise had turned to worry. He'd wake with one hell of a cramp if he'd sat in that position for most of the eight hours she'd been asleep. Feeling groggy, she must've made a sound when she sat up because he immediately woke up. He'd fed her chicken soup and dry toast, followed by a cup of herbal tea, after which he'd helped her to the bathroom and back to bed.

That tender, almost loving side of him had seriously undermined her willpower, but she'd been determined to stick to her plans of leaving for New York, especially with Ian now in the picture.

Her plan had been on schedule, until her boss called to tell her he was sending David Mancini in her place. She wasn't well and needed to look after herself, her conscientious boss informed her. Unfortunately, with Enzo in the room at the time she could hardly have told her boss she needed to get away as quickly as possible because she feared a broken heart. By the time she'd recovered, it had been too late to change her boss's mind.

So here she was, still in LA and in a chauffeur-driven car with Enzo beside her on the way to the belated birthday surprise he'd planned for her.

"So where are you taking me?" she asked. He just smiled and reached for her hand. "Why won't you tell me?" she pressed.

"I told you, it's a surprise."

"Okay, tell me this. Why the car and driver?"

"I don't intend to drink and drive."

***

Enzo tried not to think of the night ahead. His mind still reeled from what his sister had told him. He shrugged mentally and tried not to let images crowd his brain. Everyone had a wish, a fantasy. He was about to make Lexi's come true, despite everything inside him screaming for him to take her and run in the other direction.

Just before he rang her doorbell, he'd called *La Rambla*. Everything was in place.

"Will you at least give me a clue?" The slight note of panic in her voice made him glance at her again. Maybe this surprise wasn't such a great idea. What if it backfired on him?

He wasn't so hot on surprises himself so he understood.

According to Cara, *La Rambla* was the best salsa club in LA. He tried not to think about the other thing she'd told him. He'd done his own investigating and, frankly, things could go either way. Lexi would either love it or hate it. Glancing at her, he decided to come clean. Somewhat.

"Salsa," he said.

Her eyes widened, but after a moment they lost their haunted look. He knew his insensitive quip about drinking and driving had hurt her, and he felt like a heel. Raising her hand, he kissed the back of it.

"You're taking me to a salsa club?" she asked.

"Yeah."

"But...why?"

"Why not? You love salsa."

"I know, but…don't you think you're taking this thing a bit too far? You stayed in my apartment all week looking after me, now you're doing this?"

He frowned. "What's wrong with that?" Wasn't that what boyfriends and husbands did, take care of their women?" If tragedy and betrayal hadn't derailed them, they'd be married by now, even started a family. Bitterness and a whole load of regret twisted inside him, but he pushed it away. Tonight wasn't about dwelling on the past. It was about giving his woman what she wanted and moving to embrace the future, hopefully with her at his side.

"What's wrong is that we're not a couple anymore, remember? You don't have to do this. We can always go back home, order take out?" Hope lightened her voice.

Hell, no. He couldn't have turned back if he tried. After what his sister had told him, he needed to know. "Relax," he said. Whether to reassure himself or her, he wasn't so sure.

"Tell me what's going on," she demanded.

He kept his gaze straight ahead. "I told you, we're going to a salsa club."

"Did you ever stop to think I don't dance anymore? Or even like salsa?"

His eyes whipped back to hers. "If that's true, then the night's wasted. Is it?" he asked when she said nothing.

"Well, I haven't danced in a…while. Over a year, to be exact."

Since the accident, she meant. For some reason, the admission both pleased and saddened him. But he wasn't going to dwell on the past, he repeated to himself.

"So, maybe it's time to make up for it." His hand settled on his thigh and, from the corner of his eye, he saw her follow the movement. His own eyes traced her fishnet-covered thighs and shifted to ease the instant hard-on. Nothing would've pleased him more than to ask the driver to turn around and take them home. After a week without sex, he was jonesing for some serious horizontal salsa. But—

"So where's this place?"

He grinned, pleased to hear the panic had left her voice. "That part, I'm not revealing. You'll find out soon enough."

***

The lights turned green, and their driver took the intersection into downtown LA. Lexi looked out the window, frantically trying to think which salsa places she'd seen around town. Since leaving London, she'd lost interest in her much-loved hobby. She turned her head when Enzo slid a CD into the sound system. Throbbing salsa music filled the car. Anticipation heated her blood. Against her will, the music suffused her senses, bringing with it memories of dancing with Enzo.

She looked up to find his heated gaze on her. He was remembering too. She gripped her seat to stop herself from doing anything foolish, like blurting out "remember when?"

"So, have you been to this place before?" Although she didn't want to know whether he'd been there with another woman, she couldn't stop herself from asking.

"No."

"Then…?"

"A little bird told me about it."

Bird as in a *bird* he knew intimately?

"No, nothing like that."

"You read minds now?" She sure as hell didn't want him to read hers and find out how often she'd obsessed about who he'd been with before she'd arrived in LA, or if he saw other women when he wasn't with her. They never spoke about that – another of the no-go areas in their relationship.

"Not as much as I'd like to."

"What's that supposed to mean?"

"Well, for one thing I'd love to be able to get inside your head and find out what the last couple of weeks have been all about. You didn't return my calls, didn't want to meet up, and you turned nasty when I showed up on your doorstep."

"I didn't turn nasty. Not even when you accused me of seeing Ian Pulbrook." She turned her face away, so he wouldn't see how that had hurt.

"No, there was something going on with you even before I confronted you about Pulbrook. He hasn't been in touch, has he?" he tagged on with a tight voice.

The last person she wanted to talk about was Ian Pulbrook. "You know he hasn't. You've been in my apartment all week." And as far as she knew, the crank calls had stopped. She hadn't received any more calls after Enzo answered her phone and told her there was no one on the line.

"Good."

Silence reigned for a few minutes.

"So?" he prompted.

"What?"

"Is something bothering you? Tell me."

"No."

"No you're not telling me, or no, nothing's bothering you?"

"How about, I just want to enjoy this…this thing you're cooking up and not think about anything else?"

He eyed her for several seconds, and then nodded. "That works for me. But sooner or later, you'll have to tell me."

She breathed a sigh of relief when he turned the music up and pulled her close. A few minutes later, they pulled up in front of a very large, square, red-bricked building. From the outside, ivy creepers clung to the three-storey and within the vines, red and gold lights had been strung to create a stunning effect.

On one side, *La Rambla* was displayed in bold red, neon piping. Two rows of large palms lined the entrance. Enzo helped her out as the driver waited in line for the valet and, with every swing of the huge wooden doors that led into the club, the heavy beat of conga drums reached her ears.

When they reached the door, he turned to her. "You ready?"

No, she wasn't. "Sure."

A large bouncer lifted the rope for them to enter the foyer. He took the gold embossed card Enzo handed over and peered at it. "Through the doors, turn right, and up the stairs, sir. Rita, your hostess, will escort you to your private room."

"Private room?" Either Enzo ignored her question or the loud music masked her words. Either way, she didn't press him any further.

Because the music entranced her, as did the décor. In a rich blend of Spanish, Cuban, and Mexican art, the walls were decorated with mahogany beams and pictures of famous salsa aficionados from all three countries. She spied Francisco Vasquez, Celia Cruz, hailed as the queen of salsa, Tito Puente, and a black and white sketch of Arsenio Rodriguez.

African face masks interspersed the pictures to give an ethnic feel and, on the far side of the cavernous space, a live Cuban band, complete with the conga drums she'd heard kept dancers on the floor gyrating in a sea of writhing, sweating bodies.

Excitement ratcheted through her. She realized her love of salsa hadn't died, just been buried underneath the pain of her life. Just for tonight, she willed the pain away.

Enzo led the way up the stairs and she followed, although what she really wanted was to get on the dance floor and lose herself in the rhythm of the music.

At the top of the stairs, a dark haired woman stepped forward. She wore a short, white halter-necked dress with gold hoops dangling in her ears. Her makeup was impeccable, as was her smile.

"Welcome to *La Rambla*. My name is Rita, and I'll be your hostess this evening. If you need anything, anything at all, don't hesitate to ask." She took the card Enzo handed over and led them along a wide, curved red-carpeted corridor. Beside a wood paneled door, she inserted the card into an electronic strip on the wall.

The room they entered was lined with dark red velvet. Low lights created an intimate ambience and speakers fed in music straight from the band. Her disappointment at missing the live band faded as she took in the layout of the room. Half suspended over the main dance floor, it gave a clear view through a floor-to-ceiling glass window. Inside the room, plush recliners with fat cushions ensured comfort and, on the large low table, a bucket of champagne rested in an ice bucket. Along one wall, a low bar displayed several bottles of liquors, cocktail mixers, and expensive wine.

She experienced a stab of anxiety. Enzo didn't know she'd given up alcohol.

"Would you like a cocktail or a glass of *Cristal*?" their hostess asked.

He cocked a brow at her.

"I'll start with a cocktail. A *virgin* cocktail," she clarified when Rita reached for the Cuevas.

When Enzo's expression turned puzzled, she hastened to add, "I'm pacing myself. No need to rush it, is there?"

She breathed a sigh of relief when his expression cleared.

"I'll have a beer," he said.

Dropping her tiny bag on the table, she moved to the window. Unable to stop herself, she tapped her feet to the music. The beat pulsated through her, waiting to run free through her blood. Enzo materialized beside her with his beer and her drink. She took a sip as he twisted the top off his *San Miguel* and took a long swallow.

Standing still was impossible. Almost in a trance, she moved her hips. Her torso followed. The sinuous movement surprised her with its familiarity.

"You haven't forgotten how, have you?"

Glancing over, she found his gaze on her.

"When you give into it, salsa becomes a part of your soul No matter how long you abstain, it remains in your blood.

It's a lot like great sex," he breathed in her ear as he slid behind her. One hand snuck around her waist to rest on her stomach. The other lifted the bottle to his lips. To the beat of the drums, he moved his pelvis toward hers, nudging her forward. They swayed together, their bodies reclaiming the rhythm they'd found a thousand years ago in a salsa club in London. He allowed her another sip of her cocktail, then he took her glass from her and set it on the table with his half empty bottle.

He took her hand, led her into a double turn, before slamming her into his body. Both hands slid down her sides to mold her waist into the beat. Her hips moved of their own accord, her legs widening to accommodate the length of muscled leg he slid between hers.

Beneath her fingers, the black silk of his shirt singed her palms. God, he was hot. His heart pumped along to the tempo of the music. He twirled her away from him, brought her back almost instantaneously before bending her over his arm. She fell into the rhythm as if born to it, and the passion in his face as he danced made her want to weep with joy.

Faster and faster they moved, until cymbals crashed around them in a deafening crescendo.

When he pulled her up from another deep dip, she was flushed and her hair was in disarray, but she didn't care. She felt more alive than she had in the past year. His arms closed around her, while his head descended to seal his mouth to hers. Heart beating wildly, she rose on tiptoe and kissed him right back, telling him without words how much he meant to her. At last he lifted his head, lingered for a last kiss before he pulled away.

"Happy birthday, baby."

Her spirits dimmed at the hated endearment, but she shrugged off the feeling. Tonight wasn't about the past or even the future. Here and now was all that mattered.

Twirling away from him, she picked up her drink and took a long sip. "Thank you so much for bringing me here. This place is amazing." She looked around. "But why a private room instead of down there?" She waved to the crowd below, now moving as one to the rhythm of a rumba beat.

"Because from here, we can enjoy the best of both worlds."

"You mean, join the crowd downstairs or have our party here?"

"Yeah. Or we can enjoy a more…exclusive party. Upstairs."

The way he said the words made a tingle dance along her spine. The look in his eyes reminded her of earlier, in the car, when she had the feeling he was holding something back.

"What sort of party?"

"Finish your drink. Rita will give us a tour."

With a start, she looked around. She'd completely forgotten about their hostess. But they were alone. "Where'd she go?"

"She's close by. It's her job to be discreet. Ready to head upstairs?"

She hesitated, noting the hint of reluctance in his voice. If he didn't want to go upstairs - whatever happened there - why did he suggest it? "Are you?"

He shrugged. "We can go downstairs and mingle."

The band had started another pulse-raising song.

Again, she hesitated and took a sip of her drink, hoping for the Dutch courage which never came. "What's on this floor?"

"More rooms. Some cater to bigger parties, but most are like this." He picked up his beer and drained it. "So, what's it to be? Downstairs? Or upstairs?"

Chapter Eleven

As much as she tried, Lexi couldn't read the look in his eyes. After a moment, she made up her mind.

"Downstairs. I want another dance."

An expression close to relief flared through his eyes. What the hell was going on? What was he hiding from her? Whatever game he was playing, she wanted to know. "I've changed my mind. I want to go upstairs."

He raised a startled gaze to her. "You sure?"

She shrugged. "I get the feeling it's why you brought me here. So let's get on with it, shall we?"

A slow, decidedly reluctant nod. "If that's what you want."

"What I want is for you to tell me what's going on!"

"I could tell you. Or you can see for yourself."

"Fine." She set her glass down and ran a nervous tongue over her lips. "Let's go."

For several heartbeats, he didn't move. Then he reached out and pressed a button on the wall. Seconds later, Rita appeared. "Would you like another drink? Our chef prepares the best enchiladas north of the border if you'd like something to eat?"

"No, thanks. Maybe later. Right now we want to take a tour upstairs."

If Lexi had hoped to read something in Rita's face, she was disappointed. Without missing a beat, their hostess gestured toward the door.

"Of course. If you'll follow me?"

She led the way deeper into the semi-circular hallway until they reached another foyer. Wide gold-carpeted steps led up to a door painted black with a gold knocker shaped like a Mayan mask displayed in the middle. She rapped it twice. It opened to reveal a slim, well-dressed man.

Rita stood aside, a smile still on her face. "Diego will take care of you from here. If you wish to return downstairs, please inform him and I will come and escort you."

Enzo nodded.

Lexi could only manage a smile. The threat of the unknown veered her emotions from heady excitement to acute trepidation. She followed Enzo and Diego along another shorter hallway. Strobe lighting flashed as they drew toward the end and, as before, she heard pounding music. But the music here was much more subdued, slower and more suited to tango than salsa.

They emerged onto a large landing, and she stood transfixed at the scene before her.

Down shallow steps, the sunken dance floor was divided into two halves.

Couples and lone dancers.

On one side, couples, some clearly professional dancers, executed the complicated moves of the Argentine tango with exquisite precision. Sinewy bodies glided, buttocks clenched, and legs flicked with superb control.

On the other side, individual dancers, both men and women in glamorous outfits, danced with free abandon, their movements sensual and sexy. They swayed, they slid, and they rubbed, in highly suggestive ways that made the air clog in her throat.

The music ended and everyone changed partners, sliding smooth arms around the nearest body and continuing to dance as if they were one entity.

She could have stood there watching all night.

She looked up, away from the scene in front of her, and sucked in a breath when she saw the dancing wasn't restricted to the dance floor. Tiered balconies curved on both sides, overlooking the dance floor below. Here too, everyone danced, but changed partners every few minutes, moving with fluid grace into the arms of the nearest person. Only one or two stood apart, sipping their drinks and watching.

"This is the heart of *La Rambla*, where music takes over the senses and all inhibitions are left behind."

She jerked at the sound of Diego's voice close to her ear. The hand Enzo curved around her waist tightened, and she sought comfort from it.

"You can participate as much, or as little, as you choose. The bar is over there." Diego nodded to their left. "Or if you prefer, just order whatever you need from a waitress. The tab will be put on your room. On either side of the dance floor, there are rooms with more privacy, feel free to use them. Enjoy *La Rambla*." Diego gave a shallow bow and retreated into the darkness.

On closer inspection, she saw a couple in the so-called private room. Peering closer, she saw just what they were doing. The guy's cock was in the woman's closed grip and she had her tongue firmly in his mouth. As Lexi watched, his eyes opened and he stared straight at her.

Heat engulfed her face as she glanced away.

Private rooms, but within sight of anyone who cared to glance in.

A shaky breath escaped her parted lips. She couldn't look at Enzo, and she forced herself not to look at the dancers, for fear he'd see what she ached to hide.

"If you want to dance…or do anything else, I won't stop you," he breathed in her ear.

Her gaze flew to his, her mouth drying at his words. The look on his face sank her heart.

"You know, don't you?" she asked bluntly, fighting the tide of shame that crawled through her. *Please let him say no, please, please—*

He responded with a single nod. She wanted to run and hide.

"How?"

"Something about a truth or dare confession?"

She squeezed her eyes shut for a second. "Cara told you."

Again a nod.

Far from thinking the events of a year ago had been put under lock and key, it seemed the past was determined to keep surging up and biting her in the ass. "Why?"

"I wanted ideas for your birthday."

"And she told you to bring me here. Just like that?" She tried to read his expression, anxious for any signs of distaste or disgust.

He shrugged. "She seemed to think it was something you needed to experience. Was she right?"

"You should've asked me."

"Would you have come tonight?"

Would she? She shuddered. Most likely not. She'd kept her secret buried for too long, bore the prude tag for too long, to just expose it at the drop of a hat. Even after all she'd experienced in Enzo's bed, the thought that she was somehow lacking still niggled. But to rid herself of it, *like this?*

She turned away. "Your sister has a big mouth."

"But she's got guts. Gotta give her that."

She heard admiration in his voice. "So what is this? A test? An experiment to see if *I've* got guts?"

"Hey, you can walk away without a backward glance, if that's what you want. Or you can go with your instinct. It's entirely up to you."

"And you? How do you feel about doing me in front of strangers?"

His jaw tightened. "This isn't about me. It's about you and I guess some sort of demon you seem to be fighting."

She sucked in a shocked breath. "*Jesus,* I wouldn't go *that* far."

"So why did you never tell me about it? Why keep it secret? You're not the first person to fantasize about this sort of thing. There's no reason to be ashamed of it. Trust me, I know you're not a prude."

"Enzo—"

He ran his hand down her arm. "Shh. It's your birthday. I'm man enough to put my ego aside and let you enjoy yourself. If you need to prove something to yourself, I'm here to support you. But only if it's what you want, too."

Lexi stiffened. "I don't think it's a good idea."

"Look, why don't you start with a dance? I'll join you in a few minutes." Enzo started to urge her onto the dance floor.

She clutched his arm. "No!"

He raised his brow. "Wanna go back downstairs?"

"I…" Lexi's gaze strayed back to the dancers and she bit her lip. If she didn't grasp this opportunity, she'd forever wonder if deep down, she was a prude.

He kissed her on the cheek, then his mouth drifted to her ear. "It's all right, baby. This is your night. We'll do whatever you want."

"Y-you sure?"

"Sure, I'm sure. We both know you need to do this. Besides, what red-blooded man hasn't dreamt of his woman giving him a sexy floorshow?"

Still, she hesitated. Then, heart hammering, Lexi took a tiny step forward.

Enzo grabbed her arm. "Hey, before you go."

She turned her head toward him. His mouth took hers in a forceful kiss, his tongue delving between her lips. His other hand came up and curved over her back, his possessive hold bolstering her confidence a little. Entwining her arms around his neck, she gave as good as she got. A long while later, he lifted his head.

"Was that for you or for me?" she murmured, shaken.

His grin flashed like lightning. "Definitely for me. Because I want to kill every man in here who will be watching you dance. This tells them you're mine. That they can look but they can't touch."

With a sharp pat on her bottom, he stepped away.

Lexi felt lost. Summoning her willpower, she took a step down. And another. Until she stood on the edge of the floor. This was what she'd always wanted. A chance to prove to herself and all the men who'd hung the label on her that she wasn't a prude, that she could be adventurous outside the bedroom. Someone bumped into her. She steadied herself and realized she'd moved onto the dance floor.

"Would you like to tango, *bonita*? You're certainly dressed for it."

She looked up in the eyes of a tall, dark-haired man who stood beside her. Hastily she shook her head. With a shrug, he melted into the crowd. Her heart hammered as the music changed into a slower beat. A glance over her shoulder showed Enzo at the top of the stairs, a drink in his hand, which he raised to her. She smiled. She could do this.

Turning to face him, she looked into his eyes and swayed her hips. He gave a small nod of encouragement. She moved again, her hip movements more pronounced. Her arms rose from her sides and curved above her head. Against the mesh of her top, her nipples tightened into painful buds. The sensation felt unbelievable. She spun around, the fever in her blood rushing through her senses.

She felt Enzo's eyes on her as her torso and shoulders swayed in time with the music. Raising her head, she stared straight at him, lowered her hands and, with slow movements, unbuttoned her vest to reveal the see-through top. When it fell open, warm air rushed over her breasts, tightening her swollen nipples further, as molten heat shot through her pelvis. Feeling bolder, she reached up, shrugged off the vest, and threw it at Enzo. He caught it and raised it to his face to inhale her scent, before tucking it in his back pocket. When he glanced back at her, the passion in his eyes made her breath catch.

Starved for air, she inhaled deeply, then lifted and sank both hands into her hair. The action caused her nipples to graze once more against the mesh. His gaze dropped to her breasts and his jaw tightened. A passing waiter took care of Enzo's glass and he descended the stairs to her. The music pumped through her blood and the sweat of the dancers made her nose tingle, but she only had eyes for her lover.

He grasped her hand, spun her round, and slammed her back against his front. "So, you come here often?"

Her smile at the cheesy line quickly melted when she felt the hot slide of warm lips against her neck. "No. This is my first time."

"Hmm, an exhibitionist virgin. I like that." One hand caressed her midriff, passing dangerously close to the curve of her breast. Her breath hitched.

"So you do this all the time, do you?"

Warm lips tugged on one earlobe. "No. It's my first time too."

"And how's the experience so far?" She reached up and traced a red-tipped fingernail down his taut cheek. He gave a helpless jerk against her ass.

"It has its bonuses. But I'd like to explore further, before I make up my mind." Lean fingers drifted down to toy with her waistband, setting the bare skin on fire.

"What d'you have in mind?" she panted.

"I like the feel of your hands on me. Feel free to explore some more." His hands slid down her sides to anchor on her hips. Together they swayed as she reached around his nape to scrape her fingers through his hair. When he pressed her closer to his thick erection, she purred with satisfaction.

Her eyes drifted shut as the music took over. This was good. She felt fabulous.

When one long leg slotted between hers, she arched her back, and pressed her needy heat against Enzo's thigh. The pressure caused even more bittersweet pain to ricochet through her.

"Damn. For a novice, you're a natural. No, don't pull away. I love it." His hand drifted from her hip until it reached the hem of her shorts. "I love your pantyhose. I'm getting even harder wondering if it's crotchless."

"You'll just have to keep wondering."

He spun her around and clamped her close. "Keep dancing like that and I might have to take control of this...situation."

"So, you're here to drag me off to your lair, caveman-style? Fuck me until I beg for mercy?" The feel of his chest against hers caused her to lose her footing. Lexi clutched his shoulders and felt his muscles bunch in reaction.

"Maybe. First time for everything."

Indeed. All around them couples danced without inhibition, some more than others. The scent of sex filled the air. And she wasn't freaking out yet.

She rose on tiptoe to trace her tongue across his lips. A harsh breath rushed through his teeth. The grip on her ass tightened.

"Lexi."

The deep rasp of his voice saying her name evoked such excitement, she felt wetness pool between her legs. Anticipation heated her blood to fever pitch. Her hands convulsed over his biceps. Their gazed locked; heat arced between them. Without breaking eye contact, he danced them backward, his hands sneaking under her top to explore her flesh.

Lexi didn't know, or even care, where they went. All she wanted was to feel his hands on her breasts, caressing her, moving up to play with and pinch her nipples. When her feet left the hardwood floor of the dance area, she registered carpet underfoot, but not enough to wrench her attention from the dark green gaze holding hers.

Only when she felt soft velvet at her back did she look around her. They were in an alcove, half hidden from the other dancers, but with enough isolation to continue their private dance. A gold pole-dancing rod gleamed invitingly from the middle of the space.

On the far side, handlebars with leather straps poked from the walls. Their unashamed presence plagued her with misgivings and she turned away. A few feet away other dancers swayed, lost in their own world. No one watched them, but still she felt…exposed.

Enzo continued to gaze at her. There was a silent question in his eyes, but with it was a need that made her want to sing for joy. He'd brought her here to live out her fantasy; and he'd stayed with her. Could she take it all the way? She pulled his head down. "Yes."

His nostrils flared and a shudder pulsed through him. A few clavé steps moved them deeper into the alcove, but still within sight of the other dancers.

The heat in his eyes hypnotized her. With slow movements, he lowered his head and captured her mouth in a deep kiss. Her excitement soared, taking on a life of its own as her tongue licked and flicked against his. Enzo's hands cupped her breasts, expert fingers pinching her nipples. His tongue snaked out to lick her lips, at the same time as he pinched her nipples harder. Every atom inside her fired up and she was unsure which action caused the sensation rippling through her. Lust-heavy lids started to drift shut from the wild feelings ricocheting through her body. A couple looked their way. The envy in their gazes turned up the blaze of her passion another notch. Drowning in bliss, she whimpered.

Hot power surged through her at the lust in Enzo's eyes as he looked down at her body.

"God, baby. You look so hot."

"Pinch my nipples. *Harder*."

He complied with a kiss that seared her every nerve.

Unbelievably, he tasted even more incredible. She opened her mouth wider as he delved in, letting their tongues snake around each other. Warm, slippery, exquisite.

Hot darts of desire shot to her sex. Pulling back slightly, she gasped. Slumberous eyes looked into hers. Wet lips invited her back. Lexi went for a second dip as one hand strayed from her nipple, over her stomach, to her fly. Fingers skated over the zip, grazing her mound. He cupped her through the hot satin of her shorts. They both shuddered.

Lexi's hands moved down, caressing the tense muscles of his back, then ventured lower. A firm ass encased in expensive linen clenched under her ministrations. Needing more, she made her way to the front and grasped his rigid cock.

"Hmm, that's it. God, you have no idea how good that feels," he panted into her mouth.

Oh, but she did, because he felt glorious. Their kiss intensified. His movements became frantic. Lexi's zipper gave way.

"Ah, no panties...and crotchless hose. I've fucking died and gone to heaven." Eager fingers pushed inside her shorts as the music increased in tempo. Blood rushed through her veins, firing anticipation to screaming pitch. He found her clit and flicked one finger against her nerve-filled nub. Convulsions weakened her knees. The friction on her clit increased. She parted her thighs to accommodate the sensation. Swollen flesh closed around his fingers.

Above Lexi's head, two bars poked from the wall. She grasped them and stepped out of her shorts. Firm hands lifted her up and she wrapped her legs around Enzo's waist.

"Fuck me, Enzo. I want you to fuck me, hard. Right here."

"Anything you want, sweet thing." With his gaze on hers, he freed his engorged shaft from his pants. Teeth ripped open a condom as soulful Latin music pulsed around them. With a guttural cry, he surged into her.

"Oh!" His first thrust filled her to the hilt. The hands that grasped her waist held her still for the second thrust. Passion-filled eyes held her prisoner. Her breath fractured as deep sensation flowed through her veins. Pleasure exploded with each thrust, bringing her ever closer to the edge.

The music pounded their senses; the beat in time to their ultimate search for ecstasy.

"Enzo, kiss me. Oh please...I—I...need..."

Dark red light strobed over them. He kissed her, their foreheads almost touching as his cock pistoned in and out of her. Tension gripped her skull. His hand crept up, cupping her breast. Breathing became impossible.

Blue light strobed. Her legs locked, then shook.

Blissful orgasm exploded over her. A tight scream, which she realized came from her, echoed through their private space. Squeezing her eyes shut, she felt the head of Enzo's cock touch the deepest part of her. She pulsed around him as rapture washed over her. Prying open her eyes, she sought the object of her desire. He stood still, his gaze on her face. One last shudder raked her body and she sagged against the wall. Enzo supported her as her hands fell limp to her sides. Feeling weak as a kitten, Lexi moaned and closed her eyes again.

Gradually she noticed he was still buried inside her, hot and…unspent. She looked up and frowned. "You…"

He shook his head and pulled out of her, leaving her empty.

"Enzo?"

Something had changed. He wouldn't meet her gaze. "Don't worry about it. Watching you come was enough for me. I'll get mine before the night's through." The grin he flashed didn't quite reach his eyes.

Gentle hands replaced her shorts and waistcoat before he zipped his trousers into place. Confused, Lexi stepped away from the wall. Had he not wanted this? Oh God, was he ashamed of what they'd done? But…he'd been with her all the way.

"You okay?" he asked.

Was *she* okay? "Sure. Fine." She couldn't summon more than that.

With a kiss – on her forehead – he led her out of the alcove.

The couple she'd seen watching them earlier came toward them. Lexi tried not to curl up in embarrassment.

"Hey, Enzo." The guy winked at Enzo. His partner just smiled.

"Hang on to this one, Enzo. We saw her dancing earlier, she's incredible," she said.

"I intend to." Ruthless possessiveness echoed through his voice.

Lexi stiffened. She barely acknowledged the other couple as hasty introductions were made and they left.

She rounded on Enzo. "You know them?"

He nodded. "Johnny owns some nightclubs around LA. Club owners tend to know of each other. Good to know the competition, you know? So, you wanna stay here or go back downstairs?"

She felt disjointed, out of sorts. Something didn't add up. And the music was beginning to give her a headache. "Did you set this up? I mean to have them watch us?"

"No, but I knew they'd be here. They're regulars."

"Why?"

"Let's just say I wasn't prepared to come into this thing blind, so I asked around, made sure it was safe."

Her heart missed a beat. She didn't know whether to be touched or insulted that Enzo had inadvertently engineered their audience. "I want to go home."

For a moment, he didn't say anything. Then, he nodded. "Sure, if you want." Sliding a hand over her waist, he guided her through the crowd. At the door, he exchanged a few words with Diego, who nodded and held the door open for them.

The air-conditioning in the foyer, after the heat of the dance floor, sent a shiver racing over her skin. By the time they got to the bottom of the steps, Rita stood with Lexi's purse and Enzo's jacket.

He shrugged it on and handed the hostess a generous tip. With a gracious *goodnight,* she melted away.

They stood in silence as the driver brought the car round. Enzo helped her into her seat and slid in beside her. Lexi tried to think of something to say, but nothing sensible came to mind.

What do you say after an experience like that?

She looked out the window, barely registering the landscape as it whizzed by. She'd had her first, and most probably last, sexual escapade in a public place. She'd shed her Miss Prissy Prude name tag in spectacular style. The experience itself had been…surreal. Fulfilling, and yet…empty. So what did that tell her? She closed her eyes, mixed emotions twisting her stomach in knots. Was this what she'd spent all these years wondering about? Or had Enzo's lack of pleasure cast a shadow over the experience? What did he think of her?

The car bumped over a ramp. Wrenched from her thoughts, she opened her eyes. The driver was pulling up into a parking space. And it wasn't hers.

"Where are we?"

"My place. It's about time you visited." There was no warm invitation in his voice, just a statement of fact.

"But—I wanted to go home."

His jaw clenched, a sure sign, if she needed one, that he was displeased. "You're not shutting me out again. For one thing, we need to talk about what happened tonight."

"You want a post-mortem? Why, weren't you right there with me?"

He unclipped her seatbelt and jerked his door open. "Yeah, I was. And yeah, we need to talk about it. Among other things. So, out!" Enzo got out and stalked to the elevator a few yards away.

She scrambled after him. "Enzo, it's almost one in the morning."

"So spend the night."

Her mind whirled with the possibilities. "Won't…won't Cara be here?" Things were okay between them, but Lexi couldn't forget that it was because of Cara's meddling that Enzo had taken her to the salsa club. And no way was she going to air what had just happened in front of a third party.

He jabbed a finger at the button. "I told her to make herself scarce tonight."

"You told her you were bringing me back here?"

He speared her with a direct gaze. "Yep. So deal with it."

The doors opened. He grabbed her arm and led her in.

"Can't we have this talk tomorrow?"

"Nope." He stabbed another button and the doors slid shut. He turned and approached until they were almost chest-to-chest. Planting his hands on either side of her head, he blocked her in. "I'm dying to fuck you. I'm sure you noticed I didn't quite get there at the club. But I won't until we clarify a few things. Me ending the night with blue balls isn't quite how I planned the evening . So we're going to have that talk, tonight."

Her face burned, but she held his gaze. "What makes you think I'll let you fuck me again?"

The corners of his lips turned down and he shrugged. "I don't. In fact, I don't know a helluva lot anymore, but I'll be damned if I'm spending one more night wondering what's going on in that head of yours."

The arrival of the elevator stopped her from answering. Enzo led her down a short corridor to a solid oak door. He inserted his key, disabled the alarm and turned on the lights.

"Drink?"

Anything to stall this talk he was bent on having. "Water, please."

His eyes narrowed, but he stalked down a short hallway, which presumably led to the kitchen. She drew a shaky breath and looked around.

Unlike the chrome and glass of their fuck-abode, this apartment was warmth and light, designed with comfort in mind. Huge cappuccino-colored sofas and teak coffee tables strewn with magazines were arranged in front of a large flat screen TV. Potted palms provided a pleasing contrast to the browns and creams and, on the walls, soft lights and pictures of jazz artists gave the apartment a welcoming feel.

So this is where he lived. Where *she* would've lived if they'd married. Not surprisingly, she could see herself fitting right in here. Give or take a plump cushion or two and maybe a slightly lighter carpet…

"Water?"

He stood behind her, minus his jacket, with a tall glass extended. She took it and sipped. Had he guessed the direction of her thoughts? God, she hoped not.

He took a swig of his beer, his gaze never leaving hers.

"So, did you enjoy it?" he asked abruptly.

She didn't need to ask what he meant. It was obvious - he *did* want a post-mortem. "*This* is what you wanted to talk about?"

"Just answer the question." He glared at her, a pulse twitching in his jaw.

"It was…different."

His gaze moved to her crotch. "But you came. I felt it."

"I know. It was amazing."

His eyes glittered. Set jaws slowly unclenched. A ghost of a smile whispered past his lips. "Yeah?"

She set her glass down on the table. "Yeah, but then you know having you inside me is always amazing. But tonight, at the club...something was missing." It had certainly felt hot, special even, for a brief moment, then it was gone.

"What?"

Him. His heart. "I don't know."

"Think you could get that *something* by trying again?"

She seriously doubted it, because she had no intention of finding out. "No. I'm sure this was a one-time thing."

"You sure about that?"

"Would *you* like to do it again?"

He looked away, saying nothing, and took another long drink. When he glanced back at her, his gaze held a slight chill. "I'm not into voyeuristic sex. But you seemed to enjoy it. Hell, you were totally hot tonight. So I figured, if that sort of thing does it for you," he shrugged, "then maybe we could work something out." He paused a beat, "Does it?"

She could've told him no and ended the conversation there and then. But then he'd move to other topics, ones she didn't want to broach. Like why she'd been avoiding him.

She was tired of talking. She wasn't sure what he wanted from her, but discussing her one attempt at exhibitionist sex or anything else wasn't what *she* wanted. As always, when confronted with the perfect temptation that was Enzo, she could only hold out for so long. He could stop her if he was bent on talking. She wasn't about to make it easy for him.

"Only one way to find out." With unsteady fingers, she eased open the buttons from her waistcoat and shrugged it off. In the soft light, her nipples stood out in blatant invitation under the transparent mesh top. Lifting her hands, she gently cupped her breasts, flicking her forefingers over her nipples.

Harsh breath hissed from his throat.

"Jesus, *Lexi*!" His chest rose and fell rapidly. The bottle in his hand started to slip, but he caught it before it fell. He took another healthy slug, his gaze still glued to hers.

Lowering her hands, she slid the button on her shorts free, followed by the zipper. The material slithered to pool at her feet. She kicked them away. The action caused her breasts to sway. He followed the moment, his throat convulsing in reaction.

Enzo remained where he stood, a slightly mutinous look in his eyes. He didn't like that she was wresting control from him. If he insisted on talking, he could talk while he fucked her. She walked up to him, her killer heels enabling her to stand almost eye-to-eye. She licked her lips, her heartbeat escalating as his nostrils flared. With one hand, she ran her fingers down his arm to cup the one that held his bottle.

"Done with the beer?" Without waiting for an answer, she removed it from his grasp and set it down on the coffee table. Taking hold of his hand, she led him to the sofa. With a slight push, he sank onto the seat.

His gaze moved from her face, down over her breasts and legs and back again. Fire blazed in the green depths, but she could see his internal battle. "We need to talk," he rasped.

"Fine. Talk." She moved a step back and eased out of her shoes. She started to peel off the pantyhose. Slowly. A smothered groan echoed from his throat.

"Dammit. Stop doing that!"

She widened her eyes dramatically. "Why? I'm not stopping you from talking, am I?"

"You know exactly what you're doing."

Her eyes dropped to his crotch. "Is it working?"

He groaned again. "*Christ*, Lexi, I never figured you for a tease."

She kicked away the pantyhose. "First time for everything. And tonight seems to be the night for firsts."

Earlier, she'd spied a remote for the music on the coffee table. She grabbed it and aimed it at the CD player. She suppressed a smile when throbbing salsa music filled the room. Rotating her shoulders, she watched his eyes narrow as she rose onto her tiptoes and danced in front of him. "So, do you want to find out how long this tease can hold out, or do you want to *talk*?"

Wearing only her see-through top, the scent of her first climax and renewed arousal permeated the air. She knew he'd find her hard to resist. She yelped, then laughed when he suddenly grabbed her and pulled her to him. Her hands splayed out to steady herself on his shoulders and her knees settled on either side of him.

"You enjoy playing with fire, don't you?"

"Only if it's as hot as you," she confessed before she could stop herself.

A pleased grin spread across his face. One hand slid down her back and slowly over her ass. A playful smack landed on her smooth rump as his lips closed over one rock hard nipple and he bit her hard.

She screamed, the sound swallowed by the music. Through the damp material, his teeth continued to graze her sensitive flesh, while two fingers plunged deep inside her soaked sex.

Her muscles clenched hard, eager to find purchase on the source of pleasure. A fist in his hair kept him at her breast. With the other, she cupped his hand in encouragement, forcing his fingers deeper inside her, urging him to fulfill her body's demands. Until she needed more. With more force then she knew she possessed, she pushed him away and stood.

He looked dazed, hectic color scoring his cheeks as he panted to regain control.

"W-what?" he croaked.

"Stand up. I want to undress you."

Immediately, he stood. Bunching his shirt in both hands, she pulled and the pleasing sound of buttons popping made her smile.

"Hey, that was my favorite shirt."

"Really? Shame. If it helps, you look sooo much better without it." To confirm her adoration, she slid an appreciative hand over his hard torso. Muscles clenched beneath her fingers. She licked first one nipple, then the other, glorying in his sharp intake of breath.

His belt and zipper fell away and, in seconds, he stood naked. And glorious. She stared. And stared. The sight of his taut thighs and impressive cock made her wet all over again.

Liquid flooded her mouth in remembered taste and the hand she lifted to grip him trembled.

He took a deep breath and let it out in a shaky exhale.

"This is your show, baby. But I think I should warn you, I won't last long so you better make up your mind. Is this a peep show or do you have something more…specific in mind?"

She tongued his nipple as her hand rubbed his thick, engorged length. "Oh, you're much too good to waste on a peep show." Glancing around, her breath hitched as her gaze landed on a leather recliner in the far corner of the room. Perfect.

He followed her gaze. With a tense nod, he grabbed a condom from his wallet and dragged her quickly to her chosen site. Standing chest-to-chest, hip-to-hip, the heat from his body burned hers. To torture herself even more, she rubbed her nipples against his chest as he slid on the condom. Enzo bit his lip as she dug her nails into his ass.

"What now?" His fist was locked around the base of his cock and he looked decidedly desperate.

Rising on tiptoe, she wound her arms around his neck, brought his head down, and kissed him, her tongue eagerly meeting his. When the pressure threatened to overwhelm, she pulled away. Reluctantly, he let her go. She turned to the recliner, planted her legs on either side and gripped the headrest.

She flicked her hair over her shoulder and arched her back. "Fuck me from behind."

He remained still, the only movement his eyes as they slid hotly over her. Their expression made her grip the leather, hard. When his gaze reconnected with hers, she smiled, a totally wanton, come-and-get-me smile.

He straddled the seat and positioned himself behind her. Slightly unsteady hands disposed of her top, then slid from the small of her back to her stomach. His breath hissed as the scent of her arousal washed over them.

Lexi's eyes drifted shut when she felt the head of his cock against her entrance.

God, she'd missed him so much this last week. From the way he panted urgently, he'd missed her too. Obviously, the episode in the club had done nothing for him. Large hands closed over her breasts, and he surged into her.

"*Jesus*! Fuck!" he groaned.

"*Yes.*" Sweet Lord, he felt fabulous inside her.

Their groans mingled with the sultry music. His chest covered her back and with every thrust, she felt his heartbeat echo hers. Bending closer, his head aligned with hers, his breath gasping in her ear as he thrust harder.

"This is what turns me on, baby. Having you to myself, hearing those hot little sounds you make as I fuck you. I live for that. I can't survive without it."

The heartfelt power of his words rocked her. She wanted to respond but she felt too vulnerable to risk saying anything without revealing her true feelings.

So she reached back, clutched his head with one hand and moaned as her senses sharpened, focusing on the promise of ecstasy. Her muscles clenched around him and he jerked once. Lexi ground her ass against him, faster, faster. Then she was lost. The hand she clenched on the leather convulsed uncontrollably.

One strong arm clamped around her middle and he groaned again as he continued to pump inside her. "Oh! Oh God, Lexi! *Shit.*"

She felt him come, hot and furious, his cock thickening and jerking as he spent himself inside her. For a second, she wondered how it would've felt without the condom, skin against skin, shooting his seed straight into her womb.

A bead of sweat dripped onto her cheek, dissolving the thought. Soft kisses followed as his spasms ceased.

"So," he whispered roughly when he could speak again, "what's the verdict? Is the sex better outside or inside?" His tone relayed a slight tension.

She twisted and met his lips in an open-mouthed, tongue-caressing kiss. "Inside." His still hard cock jerked inside her once, twice. She gasped. "Definitely inside."

He relaxed, gave a husky chuckle. "Good answer."

Chapter Twelve

An hour later, Lexi jerked awake and blinked, disoriented. A soft snore and the arm clamped around her waist refreshed her memory. Drained after sex, Enzo had carried her into the bathroom and all but propped her up as they showered.

Now, she felt invigorated, as if living out her fantasy had somehow set her free. A smile curved her lips as she turned toward Enzo. In sleep, his face was relaxed, almost boyish. A glance down disproved the notion, for he was all man.

She reached for him. His eyes sprang open and, for a second, he just stared at her. Her hands curled more firmly around his hardening erection. He moaned, but when she caressed him further, he pulled away.

"No, Lexi. Much as I want to make love again, we're going to have that talk. Right now."

She froze. "I don't want to."

What she wanted was to have one last time with him before she left. They had to talk, she knew that now. She couldn't just leave LA without some sort of goodbye, even though it sounded tempting. But she wanted to postpone the inevitable for as long as possible. Sliding closer, she tried again.

"Dammit, quit doing that!" He pulled himself out of reach, but his cock swelled all the same.

"Why?"

"Because something's going on with you. Something you don't want to tell me about." He frowned, and then his gaze dropped to her belly. "Are—are you pregnant?

The image his question conjured up stopped her breath. Images she'd blocked out since the accident tumbled through her mind, torturing and wounding with their impossibility.

While engaged, they'd never spoken of starting a family, but she'd always assumed they would. She'd spent hours thinking up baby names and imagining what their children would look like. Of course, that would never happen now. The triple precaution of the Pill, condoms, and her imminent departure would see to that.

"No, I'm not pregnant."

"So what is it? Fuck, Lexi, why have you been avoiding me lately?"

She heaved a deep breath and moved away. "Because I can't go on like this any more."

He sprang off the bed, his erection subsiding as he glared down at her.

"What the fuck are you talking about?"

"Just what I said. This thing between us, I—I'm ending it."

Shock froze his features. "Why? Is it because of Cara? I thought you two sorted things out? I know she came to see you, to clear the air."

"Yes, she did. Which is why—"

"You mean now that you've sorted things out with her, you're walking away? *I* don't matter?" He sounded hurt, which confused her even more.

"This thing was never meant to last. You were punishing me for what I did to your sister."

A dark flush crept up his neck, but his jaw clenched. "Yeah? And you? What were your reasons for taking my *punishment?*"

"I needed—It was just sex."

He pulled on a pair of boxers. "Maybe at the beginning, but not any more, we both know that."

"So what's this now, then, if not just sex?"

Expecting him to be defensive, he relaxed, which surprised her. "That's what I've been wanting to talk to you about. Cara said—"

"Do you and your sister tell each other everything?"

"Only the important things. Maybe you could learn something from her."

"Well, I don't have that luxury of confiding in a brother or sister since you know I'm an only child. My parents died before they could have more children, remember?"

He reached out a hand to her. "So talk to me, confide in me," he said softly. "Whatever is wrong, give me a chance to make it better."

This caring, softer side of Enzo was throwing Lexi for a loop because she was in serious danger of giving in to it, and that scared the hell out of her. Gathering the sheets around her, she moved to the side of the bed.

"I thought we were talking."

His arm dropped to his side. "I mean about the accident. Maybe it'll help you move on."

"What's there to talk about? I drank when I shouldn't have, killed one friend, put another in a coma, and disfigured the third." She got off the bed and hunted for something to cover herself with.

He caught her elbows and forced her to look at him. "The accident wasn't your fault. I think you've paid enough for that. It's time to let go."

She frowned. "What are you saying?"

"Fiona's forgiven you. Cara came to see you to make peace. I know she sees things a lot clearer now than she did a year ago. You two can put all this behind you. So, maybe it's time *you* forgive yourself."

What about you? She noticed he hadn't included himself in the absolution. The realization ripped her apart. She turned away to hide the pain. "Yeah well, forgiveness might be easy for some and maybe, just maybe, in time I might to learn to do that, but how do I forget? Do you have a solution for that? When I lie awake at night thinking I should never have touched that drink, wondering if I'll ever forget? Do you have a numbing potions for that?"

"No, but the memory will fade with time and forgiveness. You just have to learn to live with it."

Easy for you to say. "What a birthday this is turning out to be, huh?" She was dying to change the subject, to get away from even more heartrending memories. Yes, Cara and Fiona may have forgiven her, but *his* forgiveness, *his* love, was what she wanted above all else. What use was forgiving herself, if she still walked away with her heart broken in a million little pieces?

"It's a good place to start. I want us to—" He stopped and muttered a curse when his bedside phone rang. Stalking to the stand, he swept it up.

"Yes? Cara, I can't talk right—"

He stopped and listened. From where she stood, Lexi could hear the pained excitement in Cara's voice.

"Slow down and tell me why?" Enzo bit out, impatience stamped on his face.

In the silence of the room, Lexi heard her screech, "*Just do it.*"

With jerky movements, he grabbed the remote and aimed at the TV.

Surprised, Lexi turned to watch the screen.

The face plastered on LA's Channel Four news stopped her breath as the voice of the newsreader echoed in the room.

To recap our breaking news this morning, British movie producer Ian Pulbrook was arrested an hour ago on allegations of rape and assault. He's being held based on the accusations of two women, one of them the actress Suzanne Baines, the leading lady in his new movie, and Rebecca Staunton, another actress. When questioned by our reporter on his way to the police station, Pulbrook denied the allegations. His lawyers say he will be posting bail immediately, pending arraignment on Monday. We will bring you any further news as soon as we have it...

She sank onto the bed. Cold shivers racked her body. Beside her, Enzo muted the sound.

"I've seen it, Cara. Is Hopkirk there with you? Good, okay try and go back to sleep. I'll call you in the morning." He hung up and turned to her.

"Do you believe that—hey, what's wrong? You're as white as a sheet."

She shook her head, unable to speak.

"You're not getting sick again, are you?"

The insane desire to laugh hysterically, bubbled up. She swallowed it down. "N-no. I'm not getting sick again."

"Then what?" His gaze went to the screen, where Ian Pulbrook's face was displayed in hi-def widescreen. "You're upset because of *him*? If you want my opinion, the asshole's had it coming. Even if the accusations turn out to be false, a couple of days in the slammer is just a taste of the justice he deserves after what he did to my baby sister."

Another hysterical laugh threatened to choke her.

He heard the sound and rounded on her. "You think this is funny?" Anger blazed in his eyes.

"No, Enzo. Funny is the last word I'd use for this situation."

He threw down the remote in disgust. "I know you two had a thing going before we met, but don't expect me to feel any sympathy for him. He deserves what's coming to him and worse."

Another shiver, harder this time, juddered through her frame. "Whatever there was between us finished years ago." With numb fingers, she picked up her shorts.

"Yeah, right," he sneered.

She looked up. "What's that supposed to mean?"

"It means you can quit lying to me. I know all about you and that jerk."

"What about me and Ian?"

"Enough with the goddamn pretense, Lexi. I know you fucked him while my sister lay in the hospital, dumped and disfigured!" Bitterness coated his voice.

Ice surged through her veins, freezing her blood. Through frozen lips, she muttered, "And how do you know this?"

"Because I saw you two with my own eyes, that's how. So don't bother denying it."

"You—you saw us?"

"Going at it like crazed rabbits, two days after the accident."

The shorts slid out of her nerveless fingers. "You came to Ian's apartment?"

"Yes," he bit out, his jaw clenched and his movements jerky as he pulled on his trousers.

"And you left?"

He sucked in a breath. "Why? Should I have stayed? Sorry, I told you I'm not a Peeping Tom and I'm not into fucking group sports."

"You saw me. And you left," she whispered, feeling numb and devoid of every scrap of emotion.

"I already said so, didn't I? You seemed to be enjoying yourself, especially with that little bondage thing you had going on. He with his hand clamped over your mouth and you doing the terrified virgin thing. I guess he enjoys that more than I do; makes him feel like a man, does it?"

"You left." Something close to horror rose inside and her body shuddered as dark pain blurred her vision.

"Dammit, that's what I said. Why do you keep on repeating it?" He started pacing.

Her eyelids felt heavy, almost leaden, as she lifted her head to look at him. She shuddered again and her hands clamped around her middle, holding herself in.

"Because what you saw wasn't two people having sex, Enzo. What you saw, and did nothing about, was Ian Pulbrook taking what belonged to me. Without my permission."

He froze. "Without your permission…what the hell are you talking about?"

"Ian Pulbrook raped me."

Chapter Thirteen

Enzo jerked to a stop. "What the hell are you talking about?"

"I think you heard me. Ian Pulbrook raped me, two days after the accident."

"That's bullshit! He was engaged to marry my sister."

Her shoulders slumped. "Oh, well, that's all right, then."

"For *Chrissakes*, you know what I'm trying to say."

"No actually, I don't. Are you saying that because Ian was going to marry your sister, he didn't rape me, or the fact that he was engaged to Cara makes him incapable of rape? If you don't believe me Enzo, just say so. I don't care."

Enzo heard her words, but her expression told a different story. She cared. The devastation in her eyes told him she couldn't possibly be lying about this, but still… Icy dread seized his body. If it was true…*Jesus, what had he done?*

He rounded the bed and took her chin in his hand. "Tell me it's not true. *Lexi, please, tell me!*"

She just looked at him with sad, bruised eyes. Dropping his hand, he took a shocked step back.

She'd been raped!

And he…what the hell had he done?

For six months, he'd locked her into a sordid tryst, slaking his body on hers in punishment for something she hadn't done. He'd mistaken the hell he'd glimpsed in her eyes as guilt for her part in his sister's accident, when all along she'd been carrying a different burden.

Jesus. He scraped both hands through his hair, barely registering their trembling.

"Pulbrook *raped* you?" He could scarcely form the words. Now that he'd put a different interpretation on what he'd seen, his mind supplied the corroborative evidence and came up with the damning verdict.

His eyes flew back to the screen, to the face of his vilest enemy. He wanted to reach into the TV, grab the asshole, and tear him from limb to limb.

He shuddered. Dear God, he'd seen her being raped, and he'd walked away. *He'd walked away.* He swayed on his feet. Through the haze threatening to blind him, he saw Lexi reach out a hand.

"Enzo—"

He tried to make sense of it and failed. "Did...did you report him to the police?" He knew the answer before she responded, since they'd named the women who'd accused Pulbrook.

She dropped her arm and looked away. "No."

He hauled her up to face him, knowing his anger at her was totally misplaced but unable to help himself. "Why the hell not?"

"I—I threatened to, when he—when he started... He just laughed and said no one would believe me. I'd just escaped a DUI charge. Everyone thought I'd gotten away without punishment, including the police. I don't think their sympathy level would've been very high. Besides, it wasn't a secret that Ian and I dated before he met Cara; all his friends and mine knew we'd been seeing each other. He...he said he'd tell the police we were both on the rebound from broken relationships, that we...we were comforting each other. It—it sounded too plausible to put myself through the aggravation. Besides, I didn't want Cara to find out."

His hands tightened on her arms. "For fuck's sake, Lexi, what were you doing at his apartment in the first place?"

"I went to ask him to reconsider breaking things off with Cara. I knew she loved him, and I thought he loved her."

"What did he say?"

She shook her head.

"Tell me," he insisted.

"He said he couldn't be seen with...a freak. He suggested we get back together. I told him to go to hell, and he...he just laughed. When I tried to leave...he grabbed me—"

"Dammit, you should've come to me!" The look in her eyes shamed him. "Or gone to the police," he amended. "You let the slime ball get away with *rape!*"

"So did you!"

He felt the blood leach from his veins. His legs gave way underneath him and he sagged onto the bed.

She immediately grasped his arm, her face twisting in remorse. "I'm sorry, I shouldn't have said that. I didn't mean it."

Weak with guilt and self-disgust, he waved her away. "But you're right. I deserved that and more." Thinking about it made him want to flay himself.

Tears sprang into her eyes. "No you didn't. You saw something and interpreted it one way. You knew Ian and I were friends and, as you said, he was engaged to your sister. The last thing you'd have thought of was…was that."

His fists clenched. "Hell, I knew I should've gone with my first instinct."

"Which was?"

"Grab him by the throat and throttle the living shit out of him."

The look in her eyes said she wished to God he had. Pain chomped on his gut.

"I guess that clarifies one thing," she said huskily.

"What?"

"Why you broke off our engagement without explanation. I thought it was because of my part in the accident, but it wasn't, was it?"

Shame made him glance away. God! That was something else he had to live with, on top of everything he'd done to hurt her.

"Lexi, I'm...*Jesus*, I'm so sorry—"

She cut him off with a feeble wave. "What were *you* doing there?"

His lips tightened. "Cara asked me to return her engagement ring and his keys. I knew he was home, so when he didn't answer the door, I let myself in. I'd decided to have a man-to-man talk with the little shit anyway, give him a few pointers on how and when to break up with a woman. But—" he cursed.

"But?"

He exhaled sharply. "Seeing you there, spread beneath him, thinking you'd both been so into it you hadn't heard the doorbell... God, I knew if I took a step into the room, I'd be hauled out of there with both your blood on my hands. Cara needed me; I had to keep a level head." He raked a hand through his hair. "But I let you down instead."

"It's all right. You didn't know, Enzo."

"No, it's not all right! Stop trying to let me off the hook."

"Maybe it'll help you forgive yourself."

"I'll never forgive myself, *never!*"

"Remember what you said to me just before Cara called? Carrying that sort of guilt around would just end up eating you alive--take over your life and not in a good way. Take it from someone who knows."

"The accident wasn't your fault, Lexi."

"Maybe not entirely. But if I hadn't had that drink, maybe—"

He got off the bed, dropped to his knees in front of her and placed a finger over her lips. "Shh. Let it go—"

"But how can I? That one drink was the equivalent of three shots of vodka, did you know that?"

His gaze rested on her. "No, did you?"

She paused. "No. Cara told me she asked the bartender to make that last round of drinks stronger, because he'd been watering them down all night."

"See? It was just a horrible mistake." He ran his hands down her arms, tracing her scar before he bent to kiss it. Goose bumps washed over her skin. "Baby, we can't live our lives by ifs and maybes, you said so yourself—"

She shuddered. "I *hate* that name," she said vehemently.

He frowned. "What name?"

"*Baby.* You started using it when we…"

He stopped her words with a finger and replaced it a second later with his lips. When he eased back, he saw fresh tears in her eyes. "I'll never call you that again. I promise, Lexi. Is that better?" He'd do anything, *anything* to make her feel better.

She nodded. "Much."

"And I'll never let any harm come to you, ever again. I'm sorry I left you with that bastard, Lexi. So, so very sorry." For the first time in a very long time, he felt the sting of tears. He wanted to curl into himself and bawl like a baby for the hurt he'd caused her. But he had to remain strong.

He felt another shudder rip through her as her tears fell. Gathering her in his arms, he let her cry, hoping it would ease her suffering. " I'm sorry, darling. Oh, God, I'm so sorry," he said over and over, kissing her between pleas.

When she had cried herself dry, he settled her back on the bed. "Stay here." He went to his wardrobe, rummaged around, and found what he wanted. Coming back to the bed, he started to pull his T-shirt over her head.

She pulled away. "No. I want my own clothes. I want to go home."

"No, you're staying right here. The last thing you need is to be alone tonight. I'm glad Pulbrook never reached you this time."

"I—I think he tried." She told him about the hoax calls. He swore hard. "It's all right, Enzo. I can take care of myself."

"You're staying here. At least until that nut job is behind bars for good." He needed to know she was all right. He also had to convince her to give them a chance. But first…

"Listen to me carefully. Here's what we're going to do."

Chapter Fourteen

"You okay?" Enzo asked, his hand on her arm as he escorted her down the steps of the police station in Santa Monica.

The three hours she'd spent there had been the most grueling of her life. But as much as she'd hated recounting the attack, the cathartic effect was immeasurable. She felt like a huge weight had been lifted off her shoulders.

She smiled at Enzo to ease the worry in his eyes. He'd stayed with her throughout the interview, and she knew hearing the details of the rape had been just as hard on him. Harder, if possible, because of the guilt he carried for walking away that day. The grim lines around his eyes and mouth told their own story.

She stopped, leaned up and kissed him. "I'm fine. Thanks for coming with me."

"Don't thank me. It was the least I could do. I—" He clenched his jaw, as if bracing himself. "Hell, Lexi, I didn't know Pulbrook threatened you for so long *after* it happened."

"I think he was terrified I'd change my mind and report him. The phone calls, the vicious text messages and emails were just his way of ensuring I stayed quiet." Thank God she hadn't erased them from her old cell phone. According to the police, that evidence would go a long way to nail Ian.

"Was he the reason you left London?"

"Partly." The other, larger part had been because of Enzo. But she couldn't tell him that. She resumed walking as he led her to his car. "There was also my job."

"Yeah. Of course." Why did he sound disappointed? She looked at him but the sun's rays on the hood distorted her view of him as he walked to his side. His face, when he started the car, was still grim. "With any luck, Pulbrook will receive the punishment he deserves. With your testimony added to the two who've already come forward, I'd be surprised if he ever sees the light of day again. Thank God he hadn't reached this level of violence when he assaulted you." He shuddered and she knew he was remembering the horrific pictures of Suzanne Baines the newspapers had leaked this morning.

She put a hand on his arm. "Don't think about it, Enzo. It's in the past now."

He hesitated before starting the car. "So, what now?"

"I've got the rest of the day off, but I'd like to go home now, if you don't mind." She wore clothes she'd borrowed from Cara's wardrobe, and she was in desperate need of a shower.

"I—I meant, what about us?"

Her heart jumped into her throat. "Us?"

The look he turned on her was intense, scorching. "Yeah, us."

"I—I don't think there's much of an *us* left, Enzo."

Shock replaced the gleam in his eyes. "What the hell are you talking about?"

She took a deep breath. "I'm going to New York on Monday. David Mancini's making a mess of things there. From there, I'm returning to London. For good." Now that the nightmare with Ian was over, she could finally return home and rebuild her life. Whatever was left of it.

His hands curled over the steering wheel, his knuckles white. "You're ending this? You're leaving me?"

The starkness of his words ripped her apart. "I think it's for the best."

"No, it's not," he said. With a vicious twist of the key, he gunned the engine, and put the car into gear. "You know that talk we've been trying to have? We're going to have it. *All of it. Right now.* After that if you want to leave...well..." His voice drifted off and a bleak look that shadowed his face made her heart twisted with pain and hope.

Tires screamed over asphalt as he accelerated out of the car park. Safety cautioned her not to speak as he drove toward his apartment.

He parked and yanked the key out of the ignition. "Out." His voice was curt, but his hands were the gentlest she'd ever know them to be as he helped her out.

They rode up in silence. Once inside, he kicked the door shut and turned to her.

"Please tell me you're dumping me. Dumping us?" His voice held a dark desperation.

Lexi fought not to react to it. "I told you, there is no us. There hasn't been for a very long time."

"Bullshit. What about the past weeks? Has that meant nothing to you?"

"Has it to you?" she threw back, determined not to be the only one caught in the emotional backlash. If he felt so strongly about her leaving, he could damned well tell her why.

"Of course it has. I've been going crazy getting you to talk to me, and all the time you've been avoiding me. And now you've made plans to go to New York?"

"You knew about those plans. You've known about them for weeks."

"But you didn't tell me you were dumping me, did you? And you sure as hell didn't tell me you were planning to return to London," he said. He clawed a hand through his hair. "Jesus, Lexi. What do you expect me to do here? Tell me and I'll do it."

Her heart hammered. "I...don't know. I really didn't think it would be a big deal."

"Well, it's a big fucking deal to me. It's the biggest fucking deal since you turned up in LA."

"Why? It was only ever about the s—"

One vicious hand slashed through the air. "Don't you even *think* about telling me it was only about sex."

He was really angry now, livid in fact. Somewhere deep inside, a small bubble of hope grew. Remembering how callously Fate had snatched her happiness the last time around, she tried to smash it down. But like a nagging toothache, she needed to prod it a little bit more.

She affected a casual shrug, even as her heart hammered an urgent appeal. "That's what we agreed to seven months ago."

He shoved a hand through his hair and glared holy fire at her. "Seven months is a hell of a long time. A lot can happen in that time."

"Like what?" Again, fear kept hope from breaking through but the new gleam in Enzo's eyes made her foolish heart race faster.

"Like forgiveness, trust, justice." He swallowed. "Like love," he said huskily.

Her shocked gasp echoed in the room. Had she misheard? "Love?" she whispered around a throat gone bone dry. "Did you say, *love*?"

He nodded. The dark storm had receded and his eyes held hers, steady and sure. "Yes. Love. Mine, for you. We've made mistakes in the past year, mistakes we both regret but have learned from. To walk away now would be to let it all go to waste. We were meant to be together, Lexi. I've fucked up badly. I know that now. But it's not too late if you want this as much as I do. I'll...I'll come to New York with you if you need time to make up your mind. But don't walk away. Please, I'm begging you."

The torrent of words made her dizzy. With happiness, joy, fear. "You'll come with me to New York?"

He nodded. "If that's what you want. I'll do anything it takes for us to put this past year behind us." He came to her and cupped her cheeks in his warm hands. "We can do it, I know we can. All I ask is that you give me a chance. Love has a great way of taking all pain away, even the darkest ones."

"But—but how can it work when you can't forgive me for the pain I caused?"

"I forgave you a long time ago. I hung on to what I thought was anger as an excuse to be close to you. I was afraid of admitting to myself I hadn't stopped loving you."

A sob caught in her throat. "Oh God. Please tell me you mean that!" Hope was breaking through. Her heart had sprouted wings, ready to fly, but it'd been hurting for so long she couldn't let go of the leash just yet.

"I mean it, I swear. I love you. *Shit*, Lexi, don't cry." Panic flared in his voice as he clasped her to him.

She clamped her arms around him and breathed him in.

"I thought you hated me. That you'd never forgive me for what I did to Cara."

"Sure, I was upset when I found out you had a drink that night. But I very quickly realized you wouldn't deliberately drink and drive." He eased her away and looked into her eyes. Did something happen?"

"Yes. I was stupid. And in a rush to get back to you."

His jaw clenched. "Because I told you to hurry."

She reached up and laid a hand on his cheek. "Because I loved you, you were my life and I wanted to be with you. I still do."

"You want to be with me?"

Fresh tears filled her eyes, this time tears of pure joy. "Always. I love you. More than I did a year ago." The words she'd been yearning to say again for twelve long months broke from her lips and finally set her heart free. "I love you more than words can adequately convey, Enzo," she added for good measure, resisting the urge to scream it out loud.

"So can I convince you to stick around? Say, another sixty years or so?"

She smiled and wound her arms around his neck. "With the right incentive."

He pretended to frown. "Hmm, let's see. How about a large plot of land, a huge wad of cash, and an architect to build us a house to live those sixty years in, with maybe a couple of kids thrown in if that's what you want?"

Her bliss-filled gasp made him laugh. "Really?"

He kissed her parted lips. "Really, but first we need to find a ring, a priest, get your grandmother on a plane, and find a killer wedding dress for you."

Unable to resist, she stood on tiptoe and kissed him. "No need for a new dress. I've still got the last one."

His eyes widened. "You kept it?"

She nodded. "As a reminder…of what I had and threw away." The past cast its cold shadow over her happiness, but for only a moment. She was too happy, too thankful the love of her life was hers again, to let it linger.

"Hey," he cupped her jaw and tilted her face to his. "No more sadness. We can get you a new dress if you want. Or you can wear the old one and keep it as a symbol of the love we found again. We can show it our grandkids when we're old and decrepit."

"I like that, so much better." Another tear fell.

"Then stop crying and kiss me."

She went into his arms and did as he asked. When she lifted her head, the love in his eyes blew her clean away. "I love you, Enzo. With everything inside my heart."

"And I love you back, Lexi. I intend to spend the rest of my life proving it to you."

THE END

READ AN EXCERPT OF BEAUTIFUL LIAR
DARK DESIRES SERIES - BOOK 1

1

CASTING

April 2015

There's no reason for me to be here. I don't need to do it.

Not another one.

I have more than enough to work with. I should end it now.

It's what I've been telling myself for months now.

Shit, who am I kidding?

Enough will *never* be enough. He has to pay for what he's done with absolutely everything I can take away from him.

Besides, I have big enough balls to admit it's become a rush. The delayed gratification is part of the game. It's an addiction. In my jaded world where everything comes to me with a snap of my fingers, risky highs like these are to be treasured.

They'll be gone in a blink of an eye. Just like every other pleasure in my life.

I peer at my watch.

5:58 p.m.

I rise from my sofa, walk down the wide hallway and enter the empty room. It's not completely empty, but it might as well be. I haven't bothered to decorate since acquiring it six months ago when my time in Boston was done and I moved back to New York. It's as if my subconscious knew I'd need it just for this purpose.

In the middle of the room, I grab the remote on the table and hit the power button. Three screens flicker to life. I sit down in the leather chair I placed in here earlier. Three faces stare back at me. The darkness and mirrored glass means they won't see me as clearly. Even if they do, my mask is in place. My black clothing and leather gloves take care of the rest of my disguise.

Anonymity is key. I'm too well-known for anything else to be acceptable. Or acceptable for now, at least. Who knows what'll happen a month, two months from now? Every day I fight my impulse. I might wake up tomorrow and decide the time has come to give in, unveil my plan.

I'm not ashamed of taking this route to achieve what I want. Far from it. In fact destroying myself in the process is exactly what I'm aiming for. I want there to be absolutely nothing left to be sustained or redeemed by the time I'm done.

For now, though, my public role is integral to my grand plan. And since my sins are already numerous, I don't have any qualms about adding vanity to them and admitting I love my other life. Keeping my identity secret adds to the thrill.

It's all about the thrill for me. Without it, I risk prematurely succumbing to the dark abyss. The abyss my shrink keeps warning me I'm rimming.

She thinks it's a revelation, that morsel of news she dropped in my lap three years ago. Little does she know I've been staring into that abyss since I was fifteen years old. I've stared into it for so long, it's fused with me. We are one. We haven't done our final dance yet, but it's only a matter of time.

I'm twenty-eight years old.

I won't live to see thirty.

It's an immutable inevitability, so I take my pleasures where I can.

"You each have scripts in front of you. When I tell you to, read them out loud. You go first, Pandora." I use a voice distorter because my natural voice contains a distinctive rasp that could give me away. Because of who I am, I've had cameras shoved in my face more times than I've had sex. And that's saying something.

Pandora—fucking idiotic name—giggles, and her

golden curls bounce in an eager nod. I suppress a growl of irritation and relegate her to the *possibly maybe* list.

"*May I feel, said he.*" She giggles again.

Ten seconds later, I place her firmly in the *hell no* list and press the intercom. She's escorted out, and I switch my gaze to the next girl.

The redhead is staring into the camera, her full mouth tilted in an *I was-born-to-blow-you* curve. I admit the lighting is better on her, but her eyes are a little too wide. Too green.

I adjust the camera and scrutinize her closer. "What color are your eyes? And don't tell me they're green. I can see the edges of your contacts."

She flushes. "Umm…they're grey."

I check the notes on my tablet. "Missy, is that your real name too?"

She nods eagerly.

"Did you read the brief?"

"Umm…yeah," she answers, her voice trailing off in a semi-question. This one is clearly dim.

"What did it say about lying?"

The *blow-you* expression drops. "They're just contacts." She leans forward, nearly knocking out the camera with her double Ds. "Here, I can take them out—"

"No, don't bother. Your interview is over. Leave now, please," I command in my best non-psycho voice, and press the intercom again.

I may be slightly unhinged, according to some spectrum my shrink keeps harping on about, but Mama, God rest her pure soul, taught me to be a gentleman. Mama's worm food now, but that's no reason for me not to honor her with a touch of politeness.

Missy's lips purse, then part, as if she's about to plead her case. The burly guard who enters the room and taps her on the shoulder convinces her words have lost their meaning at this point.

I turn to the last screen.

Her eyes are downcast. Her lashes are long enough to make me wonder if I have another fake on my hands. I sigh, then take in the rest of her face. No makeup, or barely any if she made the effort. Her lips are plump, lightly glossed. I use the controls on the remote to zoom in. There's a tiny mole on the left side of her face, right above her upper lip. Not fake.

I zoom out, examine the rest of her that I can see. Her grey T-shirt is worn to the point of threadbare, and her collarbones are a little too pronounced. Malnourishment wouldn't be a crowd-pleaser, but that problem can be easily taken care of.

Unlike the previous stock from which I plucked my prior subjects, she doesn't seem like the BDSM club-going type. For a second, I wonder where my carefully placed adverts unearthed this one.

Beneath the T-shirt, her chest rises and falls in steady breathing, although the pulse hammering at her throat gives her away. I zoom in on the pulse. The skin overlaying it is smooth, almost silky, with the faintest wisps of caramel blonde hair feathering it.

Something about her draws me forward to the edge of my seat. I like her pretended composure. Most people fidget under the glare of a camera.

My gaze flicks to her skeleton bio. "Lucky."

Slowly, she raises her head. Her eyelids flick up. Her eyes are a cross between green and hazel with a natural dark rim that pronounces its vividness. I can't pinpoint it exactly, but something about that look in her eye sparks my interest.

Hell, if I had a heart, I'd swear it just missed a beat. "Is that your real name?"

She shrugs. "It might as well be," she murmurs.

Fuck, I have another liar on my hands. "Cryptic may be sexy if you're auditioning to be the next Bond Girl. It's not going to work here. Tell me your real name. Or leave."

"No." Her voice is a sexy husk, enough to distract

me for a second before her answer sinks in.

"No?"

"With respect, you're tucked away behind a camera issuing orders. I get that you hold the cards in this little shindig. But I'm not going to show you all of mine right from the start. My name, for the purposes of this interview, is Lucky. It may not officially be on my birth certificate, but I've responded to it since I was fifteen years old. That's all you need to know."

Well…fuck. I note with detached surprise that I'm almost within a whisker of cracking a smile.

I rub my gloved finger over my mouth, torn between letting her get away with mouthing off to me this way, and sending her packing.

Sure, she intrigues me. And whatever relevant truth I need would be dug out before she signs on the dotted line, should it come to that. But for this to work, she needs to obey my commands, no questions asked.

"Stand up. Move away from the camera until you reach the wall."

She rises without question, restoring a little goodwill in her favor. Moving the chair out of her way, she backs up slowly. The hem of her loose T-shirt rests on top of faded jeans. Even before she's fully exposed to the camera, I catch my first glimpse of the hourglass figure wrapped in the petite frame. She's a fifties pinup girl dressed in cheap clothes. Her breasts are full but not quite double Ds, her thighs and calves shapely enough to stop traffic, with a naturally golden skin tone denoting a possible mid-west upbringing.

She's knock-out potential—subject to several nourishing meals. But I've seen enough and done enough in this twisted life of mine to know her body isn't what would draw attention. It's the look in her eyes. The secrets and shadows she is trying hard to batten down. They're almost eating her alive.

I don't really give a shit what those secrets are. But the chance to fuck them…to fuck *with* them, expose them to my cameras, sparks a sinister flame inside me.

"Turn around, let your hair down."

Her fingers twitch at her sides for a second before she faces the wall. One hand reaches up and pulls the band securing the loose knot on top of her head.

Caramel and gold tresses cascade down her back. Thick enough to swallow my hands, her wavy hair reaches past her waist, the tapered ends brushing the top of her perfectly rounded ass.

I watch her for a few minutes, then speak into the mic distorting my voice. "Do you have any distinguishing birth marks I should know about,

Lucky?"

The question sinks in. Her back goes rigid for a second before she forces herself to relax. "Yes."

"Where?"

"At the top of my thigh," she responds.

"Show me," I reply, although I don't really need to see it. My carefully selected stylists can disguise any unseemly marks.

Slowly, she turns around. I expect her gaze to drop or a touch of embarrassment to show, but she stares straight into the camera as her fingers tackle the buttons of her jeans. The zipper comes down and she shimmies the denim over her hips. Her white cotton panties are plain and the last word in unsexy. All the same, my eyes are drawn to the snug material framing her pussy lips.

I also see the hint of bush pressed behind the cotton.

I shift in my seat, but don't reach for the hardness springing to life behind my fly. Hand jobs are a waste of my time. I either fuck or I don't. It's that simple.

She lowers the jeans to knee-level and twists her right leg outward. The round red disk just on the inside of her thigh is distinctive enough to need covering up. I make a mental note.

"Thank you, Lucky. You may put your clothes

back on."

A hint of surprise crosses her face, but she quickly adjusts her clothing. When she's done, her hands return to her sides.

"It's time for your screen test. Sweep your hair to one side and come closer. Place your hands flat on the desk, bend forward, but don't sit down."

She follows my instructions to the letter. I adjust the camera so it's angled up to capture her face.

"Are you ready?"

She gives a small nod.

"You've just walked into a bar. You don't know me. But you see me, the guy in the corner, nursing a bourbon. And I see you. All of you. Every fantasy you've ever had. I want to give it to you. You've found me, Lucky, the guy who wants to fuck you more than he wants his next breath. Do you see me?"

Her nostrils quiver slightly. "Yes."

"Good. Look into the camera. Don't blink. Show me what I want to see. Convince me that you're worth fucking. Convince me you're worth *dying* for."

Her lids lower, her face contemplative, but she doesn't blink or lose focus. Slowly, her expression drifts from disinterested to captivated. Her lids lift and she's a green-eyed siren. Her attention is rapt, unwavering. Her bruised-rose lips part, but she doesn't swirl her tongue over her lips as I expect. She just…breathes. In. Out.

She swallows, a slow movement that draws attention to her neck, then lower to her breasts. Mesmerized against my will, I watch her nipples harden against the thin material of her top. Her fingers gradually curl into the hard wood and every inhalation and exhalation becomes a silent demand.

In…fuck…out…me…

In. Fuck.

Out. Me.

I remain still, even though my fingers itch to twitch and my muscles burn with a restlessness I haven't felt in a long time.

I watch her command the camera, her body rigid with lustful tension. Her eyes widen with the need to blink, but she doesn't.

She stays still, hands curl into fists and she just breathes sex. Her eyes water and a tear slips down one cheek. The sight of it is curiously cathartic, a tiny climax.

I subside into my seat. "That was convincing enough. You may sit down, Lucky."

She blinks rapidly before she sinks into the chair. A quick swipe and the tear never existed. Neither does the promise of the fuck of a lifetime that was on her face a moment ago.

Her acting skills are remarkable. For a second, I'm not sure if that's a good thing or a bad thing. I don't want her to be too polished. I dismiss the notion and glance down at her notes.

"You list your address as a motel?"

The address in Queens is unfamiliar to me, but the motel chain is notorious for being exceptionally bad. I hide my distaste and wait for her answer.

"I arrived in town recently. I don't have a permanent address yet."

The secrets in her eyes, the threadbare clothes, the unkempt hair and unshaven pussy begin to tell their own story. She may be brave enough to sass me when she risks losing a job that promises a once in a lifetime payday, but she's also desperate.

How desperate is the question.

"Are you currently working?"

She nods. "I work on and off for a catering service. But it's nothing I can't work around, if needed."

"So you'll be free to do this if I want you?"

The desperation escalates, then a hint of anger flashes through her eyes. "*If?* You mean I did all of this for nothing?"

I give a low laugh at her gumption. "You didn't seriously think you'd waltz your way into a million dollars on a simple three-minute screen test, did you?"

The anger flees from her eyes, although her mouth tightens for a moment before she speaks. "So it's true? It's not a con? This job really pays a million dollars? For…sex?" she rasps.

"You think I'd admit it if it was a con? What did the ad say?"

Her delicate jaw flexes for a second.

"One million uninhibited reasons to take a leap.
One million chances to earn a keep
One million to give in to the carnal
Are you brave enough to surrender,
For a payday to remember?"

It speaks even more to her desperate state of mind that she remembers the ad *verbatim*.

I remain silent and wait for her to speak.

"So…assuming it's *not* a con, how will this work, then?"

"If you pass the next few tests, and I decide you're a good fit, you get the gig. You'll receive one hundred thousand dollars with each performance."

"So…ten performances…over how long a period?"

"Depending on how many takes are needed, anywhere between three weeks and a month. But I should warn you, it's hard work, Lucky. If you think you're just going to lie back and recite the Star Spangled Banner in your head, think again."

Her fingers drum on the table, the first sign of nerves she's exhibited. "I...I won't be doing anything...skanky, will I?"

"Define skanky."

"This is going to be straight up sex. No other...bodily stuff? Because that would a firm no for me."

My mouth attempts another twitch. "No water works, waste matter or bestiality will be involved in the performances."

Her fingers stop drumming. "Okay." She waits a beat, stares straight into the camera. "So when will I know?"

I hear the barely disguised urgency and I rub my finger over my lip again. "Soon. I'll be in touch within the week." I'm not sure exactly why I want to toy with her. But I sense that having her on edge would add another layer of excitement I badly need.

When she opens her mouth, I interrupt. "Goodbye, Lucky."

A passing thought about the origin of her name is crushed into oblivion. I press the remote to summon the bodyguard to escort her out, and I leave the room.

In my study a few minutes later, I bring up the

screen on my desk and activate the encrypted service I need. I open the application and within minutes, the members of my exclusive gentlemen's club are logging in.

My email is short and succinct.

The next Q Production is scheduled for release on 20 May 2015.

Limited to ten members.

Bidding starts in fifteen minutes.

I start the countdown and rise to pour myself a neat bourbon. I swallow the first mouthful with two prescribed tablets, which are meant to keep me from going over the edge, apparently, and stroll to the floor to ceiling window. I look down at Midtown's bumper-to-bumper traffic. This mid-level penthouse is one of many I own in this building and around New York City.

Technically, I don't live here. I only use it when volatile pressures demand that I put some distance between the Upper West Side family mansion and myself. I would never stray far for long. For one thing, I've accepted that my family would never leave me alone.

I know what I know. So they've made it their business to keep me on a short leash. But with over three hundred properties in my personal portfolio, and a few thousand more under the family firm's control, there are many places to disappear to when the demons howl.

Today, the Midtown penthouse is my temporary haven.

I turn when the timer beeps a one-minute warning.

I return to my desk and adjust the voice distorter. When the clock reaches zero, I click the mouse. "Gentlemen, start your bids."

My words barely trail off before the first five bids appear on the screen. Sixty seconds later, the total bid is at a quarter of a million dollars. I steeple my fingers and wish I were more excited. The money means nothing. It never has. It's the end game that excites me.

My mind drifts back to Lucky. I turn the gem of her elusiveness this way and that and admit to myself she has potential.

I want to take a scalpel to all her secrets, bleed them and soil my hands with the viscera. I also want to fuck her until her body gives out. Right in this moment, I'm not sure what I want more.

So I concentrate on the numbers racing higher on the screen.

Half a million. One million. One point five.

My phone beeps twice. I pick it up and read the

two appointment reminders on the screen.

7pm – Dr. Nathanson. My shrink.

9pm - Dinner with Maxwell.

I re-confirm the first and delete the second.

Cancelling dinner with Maxwell will bring a world of irritation to my doorstep. No one cancels dinner with Maxwell Blackwood. For a start he's one of the most powerful men in the country.

He's also my father.

Yeah, my name is Quinn Blackwood, heir to the Blackwood Estate, only child of Maxwell Blackwood and Adele Blackwood (deceased). My family owns a staggering amount of property across the eastern seaboard of the United States and a few in the west. According to the bean counters, I'm personally worth twenty-six billion dollars.

But tangling with my father in hell is what I live for. Have done since I was fifteen. So I ignore his summons and watch the stragglers fall away until I'm left with the top ten bidders. The bids wind down, and within the space of half an hour, I'm just under two million dollars richer.

I spot the familiar name of the top bidder and I sneer. Taking his money on top of everything else is darkly satisfying.

Once bidding ends, I close down the application

and call up another list. Dozens of charity websites showing pictures of starving children flood my screen. Within minutes, fifty charities are the grateful recipients of two million dollars.

I may be Quinn Blackwood, occasional user of prescribed meds to keep the demons in check, who moonlights as Q, porn star to an exclusive few who pay millions for my work.

And I may be an unhinged asshole with serious daddy issues.

But no one said I wasn't a giver.

2

PRE-PRODUCTION

"How are you feeling today, Quinn?"

I sigh. "I'll pay you a hundred thousand dollars, if you promise to drop that question from our sessions."

Adriana Nathanson regards me silently for a full minute from the top of her rectangular glasses. She looks good for a woman in her mid-forties, would even pass for a decent blonde-and-blue-eyed MILF, although I glimpse signs of a burgeoning Botox habit. "Why do you want me to drop it?"

"Because we both know whatever answer I give would be a lie."

"Here's an idea. Why don't you try the truth for once?"

"Here's an idea. Fuck off, Dr. Nathanson." My pulse barely rises, but there's more than a hint of venom in my response, which surprises even me.

Her thin lips purse. "I thought we were past the hostility stage, Quinn. Making progress."

"Did you?" I query with zero interest. "And why would you think that?"

"Because you haven't shown signs of it in over a year." She scribbles in her notes.

I remain silent.

Eventually she looks up. "Quinn?"

"Doctor?"

"Did something happen since our last session? You appear…agitated."

I crack my knuckles loudly. "No. I am not."

We stare at each other. We've played this game a thousand times.

"How are the nightmares?"

The space between my shoulder blades twitches. Have to hand it to her. She has her moments. They're not many or I wouldn't have been coming here for ten years. Although, technically there's no cure for what I have.

I lean back, rub the twitch against the leather chair. "They're still three shades above garden variety."

"There's nothing garden variety about them, Quinn. Tell me about the last one."

The twitch intensifies. I shrug it off. "It was no different from the one before that. And the one before that." No matter what I do, how loud I scream, she still dies in the end.

Her lips purse again. "It'll help to talk through it."

"I'm absolutely sure it won't."

She sighs, lays her Montblanc pen on top of her notes and removes her glasses. I'm hit with a set of determined baby blues. "Your father is back in town. Have you seen him yet?"

I freeze. The twitches abruptly cease. Before it manifests, I sense it. The abyss. It's like a deadly virus, worming its way through me. It starts in my left wrist. Feeds through my veins and takes root in my brain. It's not easy to control it, but I give it a shot. "No, I haven't."

"And your stepmother?"

I crack a sinister smile. "That's a stupid question, Dr. Nathanson."

She has the grace to look ashamed. We both know my stepmother has been banned from seeing me without my father present. Ergo…

"How do you feel about his return?"

"Half a million."

"You can't bribe me not to ask you questions, Quinn."

"Then ask me different ones."

Her head tilts. As if I genuinely puzzle her. I know I don't. She knows exactly what I am. What lies beneath this mockery of civility.

"Don't you want to get better?"

Another idiotic question. We resume the staring match. She uncrosses and re-crosses her legs.

"I called your office earlier today. Your EA said

you left early."

"Is there a question in there?"

She shrugs. "It's not like you to leave the office until at least ten o'clock."

"Again, I'm not hearing a question."

"I was in the area. I thought I might join you for lunch."

"Why?"

She gives a nervous laugh, the first sign she's about to crack. I almost laugh. She's so predictable it's boring. "Why does anyone eat lunch?"

"No. What makes you think I'd want to eat lunch with you?"

"Because it's what normal people do." She immediately realizes her slip and grimaces.

"But I'm not normal, am I, Dr. Nathanson? Isn't that why I've been seeing you every week for the last ten years? Isn't that why you've been letting me come in your mouth since I turned eighteen?"

"Quinn—"

"Are we done, Doctor?"

"I need you to start opening up a bit more—"

"*Are. We. Done?*"

"For today, yes."

"Thank fuck. Do me a favor? Please stop pretending you know everything about me. You only know what I share with you in this room." I crack my knuckles again, a disgusting habit I've never been able to quit. I wait for her to close her leather-bound notebook and set it down on the table next to her. When her blue eyes return to me, I sit back and eye her. "Stand up." She does as instructed. "Turn around, face the door. Is it locked?"

She shakes her head. "No." Her professionalism is gone and her voice shakes with excitement. For a second, I yearn for a slice of that excitement, but what the hell. I'm about to pass a decent ten minutes.

"Good. Take off your clothes."

The prim black suit comes off, followed by her cream silk blouse. She folds the clothes away and straightens. I take in her tightly knotted hair, the gold clasp of the pearls resting at her nape, the dove-grey lace underwear, the garters, the heels.

My ennui intensifies.

"Turn around."

She obeys. Her front is marginally improved by a decent rack. I stare objectively. She's beautiful, if a little on the too-thin side. Her legs are shapely, hips and thighs lean and toned. My gaze rises to her face and I read the myriad of emotions fleeting over her features. None of them touch me. The black poison seeping through me deadens me from the inside. I lay my head against the chair and shut my eyes.

"Take the rest off and come here," I say.

Her approach halts two feet from me.

I smell her pungent arousal. She's as wet as fuck, and I wish I were in the mood to fuck her. My hands drop palms down beside my thighs on the sofa.

It's the tacit permission she needs to drop to her knees. She tugs at my belt and unbuttons my pants. Cool hands reach into my briefs and she pulls me out. I hear her excited gasp a second before her greedy mouth closes over my flaccid head. Saliva lands on my dick and eager hands rub me up and down. Muscle memory kicks in.

The spark is there, but it's pathetically negligible.

I open my eyes and stare at the white ceiling. In my periphery, I see her head bob up and down, faster and faster to keep me interested. I count the sconces, then drop my gaze lower to examine the genuine masterpieces and numerous accolades draping the walls. Absently, I count them. Twelve impressive citations.

Adriana Nathanson is accomplished.

But clearly she's getting progressively worse at sucking cock.

I sigh loudly. She bobs faster. One hand creeps over my abs and up my chest.

"No."

She returns it to my cock.

I sigh again.

I'm being blown by my thousand-dollars-an-hour shrink, one of the most acclaimed in New York City. She's bare-assed naked and on her knees with her office door unlocked. Depending on who walks in, she could lose her license. I should be excited.

Instead, I'm losing my barely-awakened wood.

Just as I'm about to push her off me, a face slides into my mind.

Lucky.

My cock twitches back to life. Adriana moans and gags with happiness as I thicken in her mouth. My eyes drift shut and the image sharpens. Tumbling caramel hair replaces ice blonde. Worn T-shirt replaces pearls. A full, soft pink mouth wraps around my cock, tongue swirling. A teasing graze of teeth along my thick vein. I roll my hips. She takes more of me into her mouth. I hit the back of her throat. She growls low and long, her membrane vibrating against my cock head.

Air expels in a half gasp. The veil shrouding my ennui ripples, attempts to lift. Sea green eyes rest on me as she devours me.

Her hand creeps over my abs and up my chest.

My eyes blink open.

Adriana.

"No," I snarl again. Disappointment blackens my mood.

Her hand returns to my cock and she attempts to deep throat me. I'm too big for her. Her gag sickens me.

"Stop."

Shock hits her eyes. My deflating dick pops out of her mouth, wet and heavy.

"Quinn? Is something w—?"

"Get the fuck off me."

She has the nerve to appear hurt. Rapid blinks designed to imitate held-back tears makes my mouth twist. To her credit, she retreats without protest.

I tuck myself back in and zip up. She's hurrying into her clothes as I stand and buckle my belt.

"Next week, same time?" I say sarcastically.

She pauses mid-dress. "I can fit you in later this week, if you want?"

I know why she's offering. My father is back in town. And perhaps the rare chance that I might fuck her. "I don't want."

Concern attempts to shift her Botoxed forehead. "Quinn, I'm really worried about you," she murmurs.

I laugh. A genuine, hearty-as-apple-pie laugh that

splits my face. Sadly, it doesn't last. It too is sucked into the empty void. "You're worried about me?" There's only a thin veneer of reason left. I need to leave this place. Now. Her nod stops me.

"Yes," she replies. Her hands tremble as she resumes dressing.

"You really are delusional, aren't you?"

She finishes buttoning her blouse and zips up her skirt. "I don't know why you're being this way."

I laugh again. "Don't you, Adriana? What does your shrink say about our little *arrangement?*"

She pales and her mouth drops open. "How do you know about that?"

I scoff at her expression. "What, you think it's some big secret that you have a shrink too? I guess I should be comforted to know you're not too far-gone to recognize that you need help. So, tell me, is there a diagnosis of *your* condition?"

The breath shakes out of her. "I…I'm not prepared to discuss it with you. Like our sessions, mine is also confidential. You get what that means, right?" She's regaining her composure. Her voice holds a touch of warning. I want to laugh again, but the whole fucked up situation suddenly weighs me down.

"Cut the confidential crap, Adriana. I started

coming to you when I was seventeen. You've been sucking my cock since my eighteenth birthday—I'm guessing crossing the line into pedophilia was a step too far for you?"

Her bravado vanishes. She holds out a hand. "You're not...You can't tell anyone about us, Quinn."

"There is no *us*!" I hiss. "And don't deny a part of you wants to be discovered. You blow me most of the time with your door unlocked, after all. The idea of someone walking in on us gives you a cheap thrill, doesn't it?"

Her pale face turns guilty. But her gaze rushes over me with sickeningly carnal hunger.

I stride to the door and wrench it open.

"Same time next week," she says behind me.

I leave without responding.

Two hours later, I'm in the VIP lounge of *XYNYC*, the SoHo club I co-own with an old college buddy. It's one of several business ventures in which I'm a silent partner because all that obscene Blackwood money needs to go *somewhere*, right?

I nurse another whiskey and watch scantily-clad girls dance below my roped off lounge. Several cast suggestive glances my way. I clinically assess and discard, my gaze searching but not finding what I'm looking for. I wonder why I even bother. Maybe I don't want to give in to the inevitability of the expanding blackness just yet?

In spite of knowing and accepting my fate, does a part of me want things to be different?

My phone buzzes in my pocket, the fourth time since I got here. I abandon my useless thoughts but ignore the phone. I'm not in the mood to deal with Maxwell Blackwood. He can wait.

I settle on a skinny brunette in a silver backless dress and crook a finger at her.

The swiftness with which she abandons her friends and hops up the steps to me is almost comical. I nod at the bouncer to let her in and take her back to the velvet couches grouped in the back. My private waiter delivers a glass of vintage champagne to her. I sit back in the seat and don't protest when she settles her long-legged figure next to me. Over a thumping *The Weekend* number, she babbles about fuck knows what. I don't speak. With her third glass of champagne, she grows bolder. She leans closer and her fingers tease my shirt button. Sultry words whisper in my ear.

I allow my hand to play in her hair as I slip deeper into my personal void. I note absently that the blackness is increasing since I gave up my attempts to hold it back.

My phone buzzes again as her hand creeps over

my crotch.

I lay my head back and unlock the vault where my darkest plans reside.

In eighteen months, I'll be thirty.

I'll inherit fifteen billion dollars.

I'll be one of the richest men on earth.

I'll also, if my plans succeed, be a murderer.

<u>BUY BEAUTIFUL LIAR</u>

ACKNOWLEDGEMENTS

My thanks to the usual suspects who make this writing journey a heady ride: my Minx Sisters, you know who you are. To Kate, my friend and editor. Here we are again, another day, another story! To all the bloggers, reviewers, Goodreads readers, FB Groups, Tweeters and Insta followers who selflessly share my stories, I love you all hard. Thank you for all you do.

Finally, to my husband and kids. Thank you from bottom of my heart for every single moment of love and support you lavish my way, and for your enthusiasm for what I do. I couldn't do this without you.

Much love,

Zara

xo

ABOUT THE AUTHOR

Zara Cox has been writing for almost twenty-five years but it wasn't until nine years ago that she decided to share her love of writing sexy, gritty stories with anyone outside her close family (the over 18s anyway!). The Dark Desires Series is Zara's next step in her erotic romance-writing journey and she would love to hear your thoughts. Visit her @
WEBSITE | FACEBOOK PAGE | TWITTER | GOODREADS | INSTAGRAM | STREET TEAM | TSU or JOIN HER NEWSLETTER

OTHER BOOKS BY ZARA COX

INDIGO LOUNGE SERIES

HIGH (The Indigo Lounge Series #1)
HIGHER (The Indigo Lounge Series) #2
SPIN (An Indigo Lounge Novella)
SPIRAL (The Indigo Lounge Series) #3
SOAR (The Indigo Lounge Series) #4
FREEFALL (The Indigo Lounge Series) #5
INDIGO LOUNGE BOX SET
INDIGO VELVET - Free

DARK DESIRES SERIES

BEAUTIFUL LIAR - OUT NOW
BLACK SHEEP - OUT NOW
WICKED S.O.B. (DARK DESIRES NOVELLA) - AUG 2017
ARROGANT BASTARD - SEP 2017